The Return

of the

Autumn Spiders

BARBARA PÉREZ

To Gemma
with best wishes
Barbara Pérez

Illustrated by
Julie Cannon

Goldfinch Oakwood Books

Published in the United Kingdom in 2007

Goldfinch Oakwood Books
129 Westbury Road Bristol BS9 3AN

Copyright © 2007 Barbara Pérez
www.barbaraperez.co.uk

Illustrations by Julie Cannon
Copyright © 2007 Goldfinch Oakwood Books

ISBN 978 0 9555151 0 1

Printed and bound in the United Kingdom by Mailboxes Etc Bristol
First edition printed May 2007

Graphic Design: Q Design Consultancy
www.q-dc.co.uk

A CIP record of this book is available from the British Library

For Stephanie, Michael, Hannah,
Victoria and Frank

With special thanks

to

Jo Whitmore
Michael Cook de Galí
and
Maria Vicedo Gomis

for their invaluable assistance in the development
of the character images.

'If you wish to live and thrive,
let the spider run alive'

(Old proverb - Anonymous)

The Spiders

General A. P. Crawly

Sergeant Steve Sparks

The Spiders

Joe Matagato

Minnie Money

The Spiders

Peter the Good

Amy Silk

The Spiders

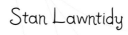

Stan Lawntidy

Karen Lawntidy

The Spiders

Rico Red

Philpot Red

The spiderlings

Stephanie Silk

Hannah Silk

Miguel Dangally

Victoria Dangally

The spiderlings

Baby Frank

Lucy Longlegs

Kat and Bex Silk

Jade Red

The spiderlings

Conor Red

Kio Red

Siam Red

Rosy Red

The General

The summer was over. In the cottage garden, the leaves lay like a brightly coloured carpet on the ground. The trees looked thin and strange. Even the climbing frame was somehow different.

Everything in the garden was quiet and still.

There was barely a breath of wind.

At the bottom of the garden gate, a small mound of rotting leaves began to shake. Something definitely moved there. Then a spindly, booted leg emerged, followed by another, and another, and another. There was a pause and then four gloved arms appeared.

General A. P. Crawly finally squeezed the rest of his body through the gap below the gate, stretched all of his eight limbs at the same time and sprang into the garden. He sniffed the damp autumn air.

'No doubt about it,' he muttered to himself. 'Winter is clearly on its way! It's time for action!'

Dusting off threads of old cobweb and bits of leaves, the General took a long look around him. Garden spiders of all shapes and sizes hung in their dew-spangled, gossamer webs – from the climbing frame, the windows, the apple tree and the rotary washing line. Dozens of pairs of popping eyes watched in awe as the General approached.

'Gosh!' whispered Stephanie Silk. 'Now I understand why he's called the General.'

'SHHHH!' hissed Minnie Money. 'If he hears you, your name will be struck off the list and it will just serve you right!'

Stephanie Silk bungee jumped with excitement from the top rung of the climbing frame and was about to ask about this list, when the General's booming voice rang out across the garden.

'Ladies and gentlemen, boys and girls of Chancel View Cottage Garden, your full attention please!' he said, tapping his gold-handled baton on the metal base of the climbing frame. He adjusted his peaked cap and tried in vain to straighten the creases in his jacket. Then he clasped the baton behind his back and performed a four-legged quick march backwards and forwards on the garden path.

'I have called you together – because you must all be aware,' he began, spacing his phrases for maximum impact, 'that winter will soon be upon us!' He paused.

'The time has come for our yearly march to find winter quarters. What happens during the next two days will be of crucial importance. Indeed, it could mean the difference between life and death for many of us!'

He removed the monocle from his left eye, and taking a fine web-silk handkerchief from his jacket pocket, he cleaned the glass carefully and replaced it.

'Our very existence depends on strategic planning, military precision, the strict adherence to rules and …sheer good luck! There is bad news and there is good news.

'The bad news concerns Mrs. P, the new owner of Chancel View Cottage. Some of you older ones already know that she's not *entirely* bad, and I must admit that we all appreciate this new climbing frame that she brought in. Both her young daughter and our very own spiderlings have had great fun with this new toy. However, we have now discovered that she is in fact – an arachnophobe Category 2!'

There was a groan of dismay from the younger spiderlings. They had no idea what the General meant by 'arachnophobe' but felt, from the tone of his voice, that a groan was appropriate at this point.

The General pointed his baton towards his sergeant who sprang into the air in surprise.

'Tell the spiderlings how many categories there are, Sergeant Sparks!'

'Four Sir! There are four categories Mr. General, Sir!' the sergeant barked, pink in the face. He took out his notebook and read:

'Category 1 – arachnophobe; terrified of all spiders; will kill on sight and therefore very dangerous.

Category 2 – arachnophobe; also terrified but will not kill spiders on purpose.

Category 3 – not arachnophobe; but dangerous because careless around webs.

Category 4 – not arachnophobe; kind to spiders; respect their role in nature.'

The General nodded and resting his baton gently against his shoulder, he circled the sundial in the middle of the lawn and again marched up and down, his head lowered in serious thought. His audience waited in silence until finally, he waved the baton over them and continued.

'Oh well, I suppose it can't be helped. Pity! If only she could be like her daughter Addie! Category 4! Now *she's* a decent type who sees the point of us spiders and is always careful of our webs. She knows we are very useful members of the animal kingdom and that we eat lots of insects to keep the balance of nature. She even stops for a chat now and then. I believe she set up a spider play box for the youngsters the other day.' All the spiderlings nodded eagerly.

'I know what you're all thinking. It could have been worse if Mrs. P was a Category 1. Well she might just as well be, because I'm telling you all now that she's got one of those old-fashioned plastic bug-catcher gadgets. Modern ones are spider friendly but the one she has is the trap-door type. You could end your days legless if she doesn't wear her spectacles, and she usually doesn't. You might as well be killed in an arachnophobe Category 1 style. That means you will be stepped on, crushed with the family dictionary, drowned in the toilet, bashed to death with the sweeping brush, eaten by the cat or sucked up the vacuum cleaner.'

The crowd gasped as the General's chilling words were absorbed. But there was more bad news to come.

'As if all this is not serious enough, you will also be aware, that there *is* a cat called Cleopatra, who likes to torture and eat spiders and who will, of course, be prowling around indoors much more during the winter months. This will make the house a highly dangerous place, so watch out for the cat!

'Mrs. P is a Category 2 of the silliest kind, a petrified arachnophobe, but at least she is not murderous. In fact, she only kills spiders by accident. This doesn't excuse her of course, but it means that on the whole, the worst that can happen, providing the cat doesn't eat you, is that you'll be trapped in the bug-catcher and put outside.

'On the subject of the bug-catcher, if you are stupid enough to be caught in it, then for goodness sake have

5

enough common sense to move your legs quickly into the dome of the stupid contraption. If you don't, they'll be chopped off at the knees as the door slams shut or you'll be sliced in two and killed as you try to escape. Death by bug-catcher is fast but painful!'

There was a silence. Some of the older spiders winced. Even Stephanie Silk sat quietly, subdued both by the chilling speech and by the anxious expression on Minnie Money's face, which she had never seen before. Every spider in the garden imagined what death by bug-catcher might be like.

'What's the good news, Mr. General ...um, Sir?' interrupted Hannah Silk as the General marched past her. Hannah, always an optimist, was determined to change the air of gloom and doom that had descended upon the garden.

Minnie Money gasped in dismay that one of her fostered spiderlings could be so bold as to question the General. He stopped in mid-march, turned, and in a flash of his baton, he hooked Hannah into space, dangling her to and fro from the safety thread she had hastily spun. She swung helplessly, just millimetres from his huge front eyes, all eight limbs desperately thrashing the air.

'The good news, my cheeky child? The good news is... um!' He paused, having completely forgotten what the good news was. 'There is no good news.

Who said there was? Did I say there was? Did I? Did I? No, it's all bad news!' He set her down gently beside the other Silks. Then he remembered.

'Except of course that Mrs. P goes out a lot and sometimes she's gone for days at a time. If we plan The March around her absence, we shall increase our chances of success. However, should she return suddenly, then you Silks, who usually winter in the house, had all better watch out as she will not tolerate even the smallest spider. The March is much easier for the Reds who winter in the garage, and for my troops who find refuge in the coal-bunker, but you must *all* be cautious at *all* times.'

The General peered through his monocle at Minnie Money who responded with a nod and an adoring smile.

'If Mrs. P catches spiders, she usually takes them across the main road before setting them free. Getting back across the road certainly has its dangers, but the silly woman thinks we won't find our way back home. Can you imagine that?' The General chuckled and then cleared his throat a few times to remind himself of the seriousness of the occasion.

'Remember at all times that although being trapped in the bug-catcher means that you won't get murdered, you could be badly injured.

'Minnie Money will explain The Four Categories,

The March and The Buildings List to the Silk and Dangally spiderlings. Peter the Good will give details to the Reds. Karen and Stan Lawntidy will take responsibility for all the rest.

'To all you Grandees here present, there will be a Web Site meeting later today to discuss the allocations to buildings. Some of you younger Silks and Reds will also need further training - *and* discipline!' He stared meaningfully at Hannah Silk. 'See to it Sparks!'

Sergeant Steve Sparks sprang to attention. Clicking together the heels of two pairs of boots, he saluted the General with two gloved right hands.

'Yes Sir! With respect General Sir, there are other matters of training that I would like to bring to your attention.'

'Then bring them my man, bring them,' boomed the General. 'We don't want a repeat of last year's catastrophe. Come! We'll inspect the troops as we talk. Time is running short! Well? Jump to it, man! This is no time to be hanging around. There is still The Buildings List to be made.'

The General strode off on a circuit of the climbing frame before inspecting the troops, who had been standing to attention in line at the greenhouse door during the entire speech. Sergeant Sparks followed the General, notebook in hand, frantically searching for both his pencil and the page on which his new training ideas had been written.

The Silks

As soon as the General and his sergeant had left, most of the garden spiders dispersed. Stephanie Silk, wide-eyed with fear and excitement, trailed behind Minnie Money until they reached their flowerpot home.

'Well! This is so unexpected that I could burst!' she yelled. 'Do tell me! What is going on? What was the catastrophe of last year? What is a catastrophe? What's an arapho... araco... you know...*that word?* Who is Mrs. P? Who are the troops that the General is inspecting? I've never seen *them* before. What is The Buildings List? What's a Grandee? Well, Minnie? Well?'

Minnie Money hated to be bombarded by questions.

'Wait a moment,' she said, for she was trying to teach a baby spiderling how to spin, hang and swing. She held the baby's finger-like spinnerets and said to him, 'Remember, Frank – the silk comes from here and hardens straight away. Learn to control it carefully and don't forget to spin before you hang and swing.'

'Well, Minnie, well?' repeated Stephanie Silk, who

was not at all interested in spinning lessons.

Minnie Money sighed deeply.

'Patience my child, patience! You youngsters of today are too inquisitive by far. In my day we didn't ask so many questions. You were seen but not heard. And you are all so... reckless!' she added, untangling the half-strangled Frank who had managed the hang and swing, but had forgotten the advice about spinning.

'I despair! I really do! How we shall ever manage to get safely tucked up for winter is beyond me. Now, ask me one question at a time please, dear child, otherwise I shall end up with a headache. In fact, don't ask me any questions at all. It might be a good idea if you go and find the other Silk spiderlings so that I can tell you when you're all together. That way, I won't have to keep repeating myself.'

Stephanie knew it would be pointless to argue, so she scampered off to find the others. At the top bar of the climbing frame she came across the Silk spiderlings – her sister Hannah, her cousins, Kat and Bex, and a friend, Lucy Longlegs. They were in the middle of a heated argument with Miguel and Victoria Dangally, who were the adopted Spanish orphan spiders.

It was rather strange that two Spanish spiderlings should be spinning and playing in an English country garden but the explanation was quite simple. Mrs. P had bought an old wind-up gramophone in a street market while on holiday in a little Spanish village called La Marina. When she returned home, she took the gramophone base outside and put it on the patio table in order to clean it, as it was very old and dirty. To her surprise, as she opened the hinged base under the turntable, two little Spanish spiders ran out onto the table.

After the compulsory scream, Mrs. P dropped the can of spray polish but recovered enough to flick the petrified pair with her duster to the far end of the patio. The duster went with them. Apart from fright, the spiderlings were unhurt and clung together, blinking in the unexpected sunlight of their foreign surroundings, one thousand miles from home.

Minnie Money, who knew everything that went on in the garden, rescued them and took them under her spinneret. They were adopted into the Silk family and brought up by Minnie along with the other orphan spiderlings. Once they had mastered the language, they had settled down very well, but they *were* a bit argumentative! They had a weird way of moving by making little jumps in all directions and they could also walk backwards. Of their eight eyes, the two at the front were very large and beautiful. They had the keenest vision of all the spiders in the garden.

When Stephanie arrived on the scene, the current argument was in full swing. Miguel had made a beautiful but different kind of web... Spanish style! Lucy Longlegs, who was the eldest of the Silk spiderlings, and therefore perhaps to be forgiven for being just a little bit bossy, towered over him, four hands on hips.

'It's all well and good to make it like that,' she snorted, 'but it's not the way it *should* be done, not in England anyway! It's far too lacy.'

'Is not important to me how it done in England,' said Miguel, with a smile. 'It catch the *mosca,* the mosquito and the ganats very, very good.'

'Yes, very good!' echoed Victoria.

'You see?' interrupted Hannah, who knew everything. 'We don't have ganats in this country. It's gnats, spelt with a 'g', but I should tell you that the 'g' is silent. I think gnats are from the same family as mosquitoes, so you can't say gnats *and* mosquitoes. They are the same thing. In England, gnats can be found in…'

Miguel interrupted her.

'Is so stupid!' he sniffed. 'Why the English start a word with something and then pretend is not there? And one more thing! I think the ganats is much more small in this country. *Everything* is much more small in this country! Now, in Spain, in my country...'

'Stop arguing this minute!' Stephanie Silk gave her best imitation of Minnie Money. 'All of you have to come with me right now! Minnie has some very important news and it might be exciting, and it's very mysterious. It might even be dangerous!'

She added the dangerous bit in the hope of speeding them up, and it worked! Miguel even left his precious web unfinished. They all bungeed down the climbing frame and hurried to Minnie's flowerpot that contained a giant camellia and a small, headless, stone tortoise. Miguel raced his sister Victoria to their favourite spot at Minnie's feet.

'I first!' he cried in triumph, lying on his back and waving his legs in the air.

'I second!' joined in Victoria, skidding to a halt a moment later, not realising that there were only two of them in the race.

The other spiderlings joined them and they all settled down around Minnie, as they had done many times before, to listen to the stories of her spiderlinghood. This time, there was no story. They could tell by her expression that today there was important information to be passed on to them.

Stephanie Silk knew that Minnie would not be hurried but she couldn't contain her excitement any longer.

'Please Minnie! Please! Do tell us. Is it really

true that the General is the biggest and the cleverest spider in the whole wide world?'

'And is the General our *own* General, for *our* garden only?' asked Hannah.

'My dear girls – and boys!' said Minnie, ignoring Miguel as he looked around for another boy. Raising herself a little and adjusting her spectacles proudly, she continued. 'The General is the biggest, the most amazing, the most intelligent and the bravest spider in the whole wide w...width of Cannington Village. But yes – he is our very own General.'

'Cool!' said Victoria. 'I think he eat all his dinner, even the bit he not like. Now! If you eat all your...'

'Yeh, yeh, Victoria,' chorused the others in an effort to shut her up. 'Go on Minnie. Please tell us about The Buildings List.'

'I certainly will, my dears. You must all listen very carefully because it's very important that we get it right this year.'

'Oh yes, the catastrophe of last year!' said Stephanie Silk. 'Tell us about that, do. What is a catastrophe?'

'*Si!* And what is bug-catcher, and what is catcher – and what is bug?' added Miguel.

'You are, you nut! SHHHH!' hissed the others and Minnie began.

Minnie Money Explains

'Before I start, children, I must say that you should not interrupt me at all until I've finished speaking, otherwise I shall get sidetracked and forget what I've said or not said. You can ask questions when I have finished. Is that clear?' The spiderlings all nodded in unison and waited patiently while Minnie adjusted her web-silk cushions and moved the sleeping baby Frank to a more comfortable position on her shoulder. Then she began.

'Now, you all know from the General's visit earlier, that something important is about to happen. As this will be your first march, you will all receive a programme of formal instructions from your teacher Amy Silk, and physical training from Sergeant Sparks. This programme will start very soon, perhaps later today or tomorrow. What I have to say is by way of introduction so that you will all have some idea of what it is you are being trained for. You need to know about The March, The Buildings List and The Four Categories.'

Stephanie and Lucy Longlegs exchanged long

meaningful glances. Minnie certainly knew how to spin out a story. She paused, had a little fidget, folded two pairs of legs over her stomach and two pairs over a branch of the camellia plant, adjusted her spectacles with her feelers, patted her hair into order and finally continued her speech.

'Now! Where to begin?' she asked herself, and paused yet again. 'As new garden spiders, you probably all think that because this garden is our home, then we stay here all year long.'

The spiderlings nodded and she said, 'Well, we don't! We have to move, but not very far. Earlier, you all heard the General speak about The Buildings List. Well that's because, any day now, we must all move into a building for the winter season. All of our names are on a list called The Buildings List. The General decides who goes where and allocates one of his special staff, a Grandee, to each group to make sure we arrive safely at our new winter home. In your case the Grandee is me. This move is called The March and it's what spiders do in autumn. That's why people refer to us as autumn spiders. We're not really autumn spiders but they see more of us in autumn, especially in their houses. You don't yet know about winter, but you will! Suffice to say that if you are not inside a building before the end of autumn, you will die of cold and starvation.'

The spiderlings looked at each other, wide-eyed. Bex and Kat, the smallest Silks, tried to snuggle close to Miguel Dangally, but he was not in a protective mood. Jumping up suddenly, he made a quick survey of the garden buildings by racing and jumping around the climbing frame before returning to a different spot, as far as possible from Bex and Kat.

'Garage 'ouse, green'ouse, coal-bunker. Is coal-bunker building?' he panted. Minnie Money glared at him.

'What? What I do?' he asked her, eyebrows raised and two hands lifted, palms up. Then, as everyone else also stared at him, he realised that he had interrupted Minnie. He clapped four pairs of hands to his mouth all at once.

'Sorry Minnie, it was the girls. They all sticky and clingy and cuddly and 'orrible. Why they can't...' He stopped in mid-sentence as Minnie's mouth set in a firm line. At last she was able to continue.

'Later, at the Grandees' Web Site meeting, the General will draw up The Buildings List and we shall all be told which building to train for. Normally, Silks are allocated to the house. That's why we're often known as 'house spiders'. The garage, coal-bunker and greenhouse marches are really easy ones in comparison to the house march, which is very, very difficult, especially when you've got Category 1 or Category 2 people living in it.'

Some of the youngsters looked puzzled.

'All right!' continued Minnie. 'I'll tell you more about the different categories but I don't want to scare you. Let the General do all the worrying. It's his job and he's very well trained for it. Now! The categories! Altogether there are four as the sergeant told you earlier. Category 1 is...'

Minnie did not get to finish the sentence because there was an alarm call from the garage roof. Peter the Good, who was on duty in the ivy that covered the garage, bounced in panic and jangled the thread of a web that stretched from his lookout point to the climbing frame. From there, it quivered via the interweb to all parts of the garden. Peter gave two jangles which meant that the window cleaner's van was in the drive.

'Abandon all window webs! Abandon all window webs!' he called urgently.

Even as he spoke, the top of a huge ladder appeared over the garden gate and within moments, the window cleaner was in the garden.

Peter the Good

Minnie and the spiderlings took immediate cover beneath the stone tortoise with the broken head that nestled at the base of the camellia plant. It was a bit cramped and also damp but at least they were safe from the danger of the ladder, the soapy water, the bucket and any other cleaning materials that would be carelessly flung around by the whistling workman.

The larger window spiders had scattered within moments of Peter the Good's alarm call. They abandoned their scaffolding and scampered to safety under the eaves of the house or to the flowerpots that flanked the entire front wall.

'I hope he will have his usual cup of tea first,' prayed Peter, knowing that some of the smaller spiders needed more time to escape.

The window cleaner rang the back porch bell and the Silks all watched with bated breath, each one crossing all their legs for luck. Hannah Silk also crossed her eyes for good measure.

'Let her be in!   Please let her be in!' whispered Hannah. 'Yes! She's in! Wicked!'

The stable doors of the porch opened and Mrs. P

appeared in her fleecy red dressing gown and red plaid slippers.

'Good morning, Tom! Is it six weeks already? My goodness! How time flies! Cup of tea?' Tom placed his ladder against the wall and dumped his bucket on the path.

'Aye! Go on then,' he said and leaned against the patio table, a little out of breath.

Peter the Good raised his four front legs to the sky as he watched the rest of the window spiders scuttling to safety.

'What a great blessing is a cup of tea!' he said. He had rounded up his flock and was satisfied that they were all safely hidden. It was a pity about the webs though, and more importantly, about their contents; all those tasty morsels of food, neatly wrapped in web parcels and ready to eat. He sighed, wondering if there might be just about enough time to nip up to one of the lower windows and grab one, but he thought better of it. Not worth the risk!

It was a wise decision, for a few minutes later the window cleaner placed his cup of tea on the patio table to cool, re-positioned his ladder and started work. Mrs. P's head appeared around the porch door.

'Be sure to clear all the cobwebs won't you Tom! There are so many of them at this time of year.'

During the following twenty minutes or so,

under the mournful gaze of the window spiders, the beautiful webs were destroyed and the window cleaning home-wrecker left.

Peter gave the all clear and the unhappy spiders returned to assess the damage and start the rebuild. Stan Lawntidy collected and sorted the web food parcels on the gravel path. He discarded the soggy ones, placing them in a neat pile on the ground, and began his rounds of returning the dry ones to their owners. Peter the Good sighed again and patted a few shoulders sympathetically before going back to the garage ivy to continue his watch.

The General had appointed Peter as Insect Service Manager (ISM) on account of his great wisdom and immense kindness towards others. His clients were not just spiders but also beetles, harvesters and centipedes. Peter wasn't paid for this work but he was rewarded by invitations to every dinner web in the garden. Indeed, with some of his closer acquaintances, he just took the liberty of helping himself as he passed by. It was very convenient. He himself never made webs because he just didn't have time. Making webs was really hard work and best left to others.

As soon as Peter had returned to his dense ivy lookout home, Minnie and the spiderlings emerged from the stone tortoise and gathered together on the longer grass at the edge of the lawn. They sympathised with the window spiders, who had partly rebuilt their webs and stored their web parcels safely.

'If you have all tidied your webs, you can have five minutes play on the climbing frame and then I'll finish what I was saying,' Minnie told the spiderlings, who raced off across the grass, only too eager to stretch all their legs after the cramped conditions under the stone tortoise.

The Four Categories

'Now, where was I?' Minnie Money asked the spiderlings as soon as they had all settled down again. They were flushed from running, and excited at the prospect of hearing more about the great move into buildings for the winter. Stephanie Silk took a deep breath to answer Minnie but she was too slow.

'You were about to explain The Four Categories,' said Lucy Longlegs with an angelic smile for Minnie and a malicious sideways glance at Stephanie.

'Exactly!' beamed Minnie. 'Good girl! The Four Categories. We'll start with Category 4 because they are the best. They love spiders, and indeed, all insect life, with the exception of wasps and flies of course. Absolutely no human likes wasps and flies.

'Category 4 people will never knowingly harm a spider. They value the important work we do in the garden, controlling the predators. They know that if we didn't catch and eat most of the insects, then the insects would eat all the plants. That in turn would lead to the extinction of most mammals, including humans. They would all die, Miguel. I can see you were just about to ask! Category 4 people therefore respect and protect us. They even attempt to have conversations with us. If they see one of us twice in succession, they'll say, 'Oh! It's you again, is it?' or 'You're a beauty!' Sometimes they even try to have really close contact. Once I remember two C 4 people having an argument over who was going to have me crawling over their hand first. Mind you, that might be because I'm a very special breed of spider, with superior magical powers to make humans rich if they have contact with me.'

Minnie paused and adjusted her spectacles delicately, giving the spiderlings time to reflect on this information. There was no response.

'Money!' she suggested, hopefully. 'Money spider? Minnie Money? Oh forget it!' she added with a huff. The spiderlings gazed at her blankly, wondering why she was so annoyed.

'Category 3, or C 3,' she continued, 'don't like us very much but will never harm us or put us out. However, they do like us to stay out of their way, so they *can* be a bit dangerous, especially around our webs. They tend to sweep them out of their way regardless of whether we're in them or not. Run into a corner or up a curtain for safety and they're quite happy.'

'Are they arachno…you know…that word?' asked Stephanie.

'No my dear, C 3 and 4 people are not terrified of spiders but C 2 and C 1 most definitely are. They suffer from arachnophobia – *arachnid* meaning *spider* and *phobic* meaning *fearful* – thus f*earful of spiders*. Now Mrs. P is a C 2 and that means she's really afraid of us but won't deliberately harm us. I feel a little sorry for her, but not at all for a C1 who is terrified enough to kill us on sight.'

'Why is Mrs. P so scared of us?' asked Hannah. 'She is enormous and we're so small. I am terrified of *her*!'

'Who knows the ways of humans, my dear? Spider fear runs in human families. It's passed on to children, and so on through the generations. Parents are mostly to blame. It's just a sad fact and very strange. I'll never understand why humans are not afraid of cats and dogs that can bite and scratch. We don't hurt anyone!'

'But we do!' piped Victoria. 'We hurt flies, and crickets! We eat them! Yum! Yum!'

'Flies and crickets don't count! They're part of the predator control and therefore quite accepted. Not the same thing at all, ridiculous child! Don't you listen to *anything* I say?' Minnie was extremely ruffled at being contradicted. All eyes turned on Victoria, who hastily covered her face and disappeared behind her brother. Miguel placed a few arms around her protectively and lifted his head in a gesture of defiance, daring anyone to make a comment. Minnie thought it would be wise to return to practical information by way of distraction.

'Now the worst kind of human is the Category 1. These people mean great danger!' she almost whispered. It worked! The little ones crept closer, wide-eyed. Hannah and Miguel glanced fearfully around the garden, half expecting at any moment for a Category 1 to appear. Victoria immediately recovered from her embarrassment and tightened her grip on her brother so much that he squealed with fright. The others, mistaking this for a real C 1 sighting, all screamed together and rushed towards Minnie for protection, knocking her from the camellia leaf. Baby Frank was flung high into the air and caught by Bex. He did not even wake up. Minnie however, landed on the soft earth with a bump, having been taken so completely by surprise that she had forgotten to spin a safety thread.

As she lay there, trying to catch her breath, the little crowd of spiderling heads peered down at her from the leaf above. There was a shocked silence. Stephanie Silk was the first to recover. She bungee jumped down, helped Minnie to her feet and gave her a lift back up. The others fussed around her, all talking at once. Minnie calmly adjusted her cushions, untangled her glasses from a stray wisp of Stephanie's web, put them on and raised her arms for the return of the baby.

'I'm all right! Just calm down, all of you! I don't want to frighten you, my dears, or cause you to have nightmares, but it is so important that you know just how dangerous The March can be. Category 1 people not only hate and fear spiders but they can also be very cruel. You must all pay great attention at the training sessions so that you will be well prepared should you ever meet a Category 1.'

'But you said that Mrs. P was a Category 2,' said Stephanie. 'That means that we're quite safe, doesn't it?'

'Mrs. P has friends and family, my dear. Some of them seem harmless, but there are others we can't be sure about. They could be members of any of The Four Categories and could visit the house at any time. I've heard of human children who deliberately try to find spiders, just so that they can torture them. I'll never understand why.'

Minnie's voice broke and she seemed suddenly clouded with sadness. A huge tear plopped down onto the baby's face and she was quite unable to continue. The spiderlings patted her knees, realizing that there was much more to this story, but they didn't press her for an explanation. She eventually took a deep trembling breath and continued.

'Now at least, you are well-informed about The Buildings List and The Four Categories. You are all Silk spiderlings and quite small, so you will probably be allocated the house. Although it's more difficult to get in, your size means that you are not so easily noticed. In a house as clean and tidy as this one, it can be quite difficult to find a place to hide, unless you're a spider as small as me, of course. Mrs. P looks for us everywhere and when she can't find us, she still imagines we are there in our hundreds. If you look very closely at those open windows, you will see very fine black netting secured tightly against the frames on the inside. These are her spider, fly, moth and wasp barriers. I understand that they have these contraptions in hot countries but you rarely see them here. It's very annoying!'

'If it's very difficult to get into the house, then who will look after us and make sure that we get in and are hidden safely?' said Stephanie, who was beginning to think that this was not going to be such an adventure after all. In fact, it all sounded rather frightening.

'I shall, my dears. Don't you worry!'

Stephanie and Hannah lowered their heads and exchanged sidelong glances. Minnie was the smallest spider in the garden and therefore not exactly someone to inspire great confidence. She noticed the fleeting looks between the girls and added hastily, 'Of course, some of the bigger adult spiders will accompany us to make sure that we're all right. They are, after all, our troops, trained by Sergeant Sparks himself. They will distract the humans if the need arises, so that little ones like you – and me of course – can slip by un-noticed. They are very brave, you know.'

'Wouldn't it be wonderful if the General himself came with us as our military escort?' said Stephanie.

Minnie laughed out loud, something she very rarely allowed herself to do. 'That's not very likely, Stephanie. It would be far too dangerous! If Mrs. P ever saw *him*, she would probably be so freaked that she would accidentally harm him in her fright. No, I don't think so. Maybe we could ask for two more Grandees – Sergeant Steve Sparks and Joe Matagato, for example. They are both spiders from the White Cross family and therefore related to all of you who have a white cross on your stomachs. We do try, you know, to keep spider families together for The March. We shall know for sure later today or tomorrow after The Web Site Meeting.'

Minnie stifled a yawn. It had been a long morning, and the fall had shaken her up a bit. A little nap might do the trick. 'Now! Don't ask me any more questions!' she added quickly, having noticed that Miguel was examining his stomach for a white cross. She knew he was about to ask what had happened to his.

Minnie took off her glasses and waved the spiderlings away with them. 'Go and play but don't get into mischief. I don't want to hear you arguing. Are you listening, Miguel?'

Miguel shrugged, now frantically pulling at Victoria's T-shirt to see if she had a white cross. 'Why Victoria and me don't 'ave white cross? I like white cross. And I never argue, never,' he added, glancing up at Minnie. 'Everybody *they* argue with *me*! Who take my white cross? You! Bex Silk! You take it?'

The other spiderlings piled on top of him, and tickled him until he begged for mercy. Hannah and Stephanie Silk each examined their own stomachs. Both had the beginnings of white spotted markings that promised them membership in the White Cross family.

'You and Vicky can jump and walk backwards, but we can't,' said Hannah. 'You can't have everything! Maybe Spanish spiders don't have white crosses.'

Minnie Money climbed further up the camellia plant and selected a curly shiny leaf on which to take her nap. She placed her cushions against the main stem of the plant, wrapped a few silken threads around the sleeping baby to keep him safe, and was soon snoring gently.

The spiderlings made for the climbing frame, but after a few moments spent hanging from their single threads of silk, they became bored and wondered what to do next.

'We could go wind-sailing,' suggested Kat Silk. Wind-sailing was the spiderlings' favourite pastime. All that was needed was a high wind and a single thread of spider silk to enable them to fly around the garden at top speed. Sometimes their bungee cords became entangled but that was all part of the fun.

Lucy inclined her head towards Kat and stared hard into her eyes. 'Yes, we could go wind-sailing, Kat. That's a brilliant idea – except that in case you haven't noticed, there's no wind!'

'I cheer you up with a yoke – sorry – joke,' said Miguel Dangally. 'I tell it to Stephanie because it need only one person. Stephanie – knock, knock, who there?'

'Aren't I supposed to say that?' asked Stephanie.
'Say what?'
'Who there? No, who's there?'
'Si, si. I sorry. OK. Knock, knock!'
'Who's there?'
'Amos. Now you say, Amos who?'
'I know that, duh! OK. Amos who?'
'Amos-quito! You understand? A mosquito! Is very

funny, no?'

'Hilarious,' said Stephanie. 'Has anyone else got any bright ideas?'

'I've got a good idea!' said Hannah, eyes sparkling. 'Let's go and see if Matagato is practising.'

'Great! Nice one, Hannah,' they chorused, and raced off in the direction of the bay window, knowing that they would find him there.

Matagato was always there.

Joe Matagato and the Mission Impossible

Joe Matagato was the only spider brave enough to make his home beneath the bay window near the old apple tree. This area was considered by the garden spiders to be the most dangerous place to live. Once a week, Mrs. P had the annoying habit of taking the garden broom and sweeping the dark corners on the under surface of the window. In her mind, if there were no cobwebs, then there were no spiders. But Matagato had learned to move quickly into a split in the wood where it was possible to avoid the force of the garden broom. Sometimes his web was swept away, but he just built a new one.

Matagato *needed* to be in the region of the window. He needed to be there in order to fulfil his mission in life – to paralyse Cleopatra, Mrs. P's cat. The gravel path that ran below the bay window was where Cleo liked to bask in the late afternoon autumn sunshine. From his vantage point above, Matagato could study her and plan his attack.

Normally, garden spiders were not vindictive by nature, and Matagato was no exception. In fact, he had a very gentle spidernality, despite his fierce appearance. He had just cause to despise Cleo because earlier in the summer, she had tormented and finally eaten a friend of his. Rowly was not his best friend but she *was* a friend and did not deserve to die in such a horrible way. Matagato was determined to avenge her death.

He knew it would be difficult. He couldn't just tie her up with spider silk, which was his normal line of attack with flies, midges and the like. This would need very careful planning. Matagato was so obsessed with his mission, that The Buildings List and The March took second place. In fact, he had decided not to go to the net meeting at The Web Site the following day. Time was running short if he was to sort out the cat before the day of The March. If he didn't do it now, it would be too late. The beastly cat would be able to roam free all winter, munching her way through the rest of his friends, and maybe even Amy, who *was* his best friend. The thought made him shudder. The furry beast had to go!

Amy tried to reason with him but it was of no use. Every day he exercised to build up strength, and after that, he practised his own special version of Kung Fu. He had watched this art performed in a television film that he had seen through the lounge window. He often watched television. What had impressed him so much about the Kung Fu film, was that a very small human had overcome five very large humans by the mere lashing of a leg. It occurred to him that if he could learn this art, then with his eight legs he could have eight times the power on his side. All he would need was a special stick. It was called a *southern monkey stick* in the film, although Matagato never understood why – to him it looked like a simple wooden sword.

Stan Lawntidy, the garden refuse spider, had found a stick for him. It was really half a cocktail stick left on the patio after a barbeque, but it was exactly what Matagato wanted. At first he could not even lift it, but as his strength improved, he was able to brandish it, first with two pairs of legs, then one, and finally with just one leg. He was elated!

'Bruce's spider is nothing compared to me!' he told Amy. 'I can do anything! I just have to try, try and try again!'

'Yes. You're wonderful!' agreed Amy, wondering who Bruce could be. 'I just wish you would put some of that energy into something more useful, like helping to plan The March for example. It's so dangerous to take on the cat. She's at least ten thousand times bigger than you. One swipe with her mighty paw and that's you finished. I shall be left all alone without you.' Amy's eight beautiful eyes welled up with angry tears. Matagato put two front legs around her and gave her a fierce hug.

'Don't you worry, baby. I'm cool! She has to learn – respect! I'm far too fast for her, the great fat furry lump.'

He was indeed fast. Amy sighed, and when the spiderlings arrived, she guided them to the nearest evergreen plant so that they could see his performance in safety. The little ones watched Matagato with admiration and total approval, and were very careful not to distract him with their chatter.

A short while later, Sergeant Steve Sparks arrived and told them that a training session had been arranged for them later that day, behind the coal-bunker at the bottom of the garden. He warned them to be prepared for a visit to the kitchen windowsill to have a good look at the dreadful spider trapping machine that was always kept there.

During the sergeant's conversation with the spiderlings, Matagato continued his spider style form of Kung Fu, oblivious to the presence of the newcomer. It took a few meaningful little coughs and frantic gestures from the spiderlings for Matagato to realise that the sergeant was there. He stopped and fell in a panting heap on the edge of the plant where the youngsters were hiding.

Sergeant Sparks, arms folded, shook his head in disapproval, but there was a twinkle in his eye. He had to admit that watching Matagato practise his particular form of Kung Fu was very entertaining, especially the back flips.

'If you were learning this art for anything else but a futile cat attack, it would receive my total approval,' he said, hiding a smile. 'As this is not the case, I can only say that I absolutely forbid you to carry on with this nonsense, for that's exactly what it is. To my knowledge, no garden spider in British history has ever managed to paralyse anything larger than a bluebottle fly, and even that was with the help of a very sticky web.'

'Exactly,' puffed Matagato. 'I am determined to be the first in the Guinness Book of Spider Records to do it.'

'You'll be the fifteenth in the spider 'Death by Cleo' record, you arrogant arachnid! My word is final – unless you want to discuss this with the General?'

'No! I'd rather not thank you. I hear you man! I'm cool!' said Matagato.

'Then you'll report to me after the training session for the spiderlings. There is to be a net meeting of Grandees at The Web Site to discuss The Buildings List.'

'I don't need to be there,' said Matagato, gobbling up his bungee line. 'I really have a lot to do and anyway, I'm fully fit. I'm not going to need any training sessions either. Just tell me which building to go to and I'll sort it.'

'And I'll sort you, my lad! You be there! The General wants a roll call and if you're not there, he'll want to know the reason why. It will be my head on the block! You'll miss out on the instructions for both The Buildings List and for the time of The March. This manoeuvre will be far more successful if we work together as a team. We need your support. It's your duty as a Grandee. Just be there! It's an order!'

With that, the sergeant turned on four heels and strode off in the direction of the electric meter box near the porch door, where he lived.

The spiderlings, disappointed that Matagato's workout was obviously over, made their way back to Minnie to tell her about the training session. They were very excited about it, but they found her still sleeping. Baby Frank was also asleep, his eight little legs wrapped around Minnie's head. Disappointed, they crept away to the climbing frame, wondering what to do next.

The Cat Attack

Matagato climbed into his silken hammock, which hung precariously below his food web. He stretched and pushed back his sweatband.

'Just five minutes kip and then I'll do fifty press-ups and call it a day,' he yawned. He glanced over at Amy's web. It was empty. She had probably gone off in a huff but it couldn't be helped. A mission was a mission! He could make it up to her later – perhaps catch a nice bluebottle or a crane fly for her lunch.

He flexed all of his forty-eight knees and stifled a yawn with his feelers. A fine drizzling rain had started to fall, covering the garden with a soft sheen and forming sparkling droplets on the numerous spider webs. The rain confirmed his idea for a lazy nap and he wriggled himself comfortable.

His thoughts wandered to the encounter with the sergeant and the net meeting. What a nuisance it all was when he was so busy with his own plans. He scratched the white cross on his stomach, yawned noisily and turned onto his side so that he was facing the porch door. *It wouldn't do to get complacent!*

One of his eyes drooped sleepily. The others

41

were about to follow, when the porch door opened suddenly and Mrs. P came out of the house, shopping basket and umbrella in hand. Matagato watched her put up the umbrella and was about to look away, when something quite extraordinary happened.

As Mrs. P was about to close the door, Cleopatra dashed out of the porch and onto the patio at the last minute. Realizing that it was raining but too late to run back indoors, she made an odd flick of both paws, and dashed for the dry patch under the window ledge, just a web span away from Matagato's hammock and web.

Matagato just couldn't believe it!

He had never been this close to her before.

There she was beneath him – his deadly enemy! He froze! He knew that if he moved even a fraction, she would notice him. One vicious paw would knock him down and then she would pounce. He would be one dead spider!

Matagato quickly considered his options. He could scuttle fast into the crack in the dark recess of the ledge, and hope that she couldn't winkle him out of the corner with that vicious right paw – or – he could attack! This was the opportunity he had been waiting for. His mission! How could he back out now? He might never get another chance like this. He had to go for it!

Very slowly, he moved one leg behind his back, where his southern monkey stick lay ready for action. He raised it above his body, all the while keeping every eye fixed on the top of the unsuspecting Cleo's head.

From one of the eyes on the side of his head, he noticed some movement in the garden. His heart sank as he saw the little group of Silk spiderlings crossing the lawn. *Oh no, not now!* The last thing he wanted was an audience, but it was too late to stop them. It was now or never! He decided to go for it, and without any further thought, he puffed himself up with a deep breath. *Better not to bungee jump – there would be more force in a free fall!*

Cleo was having a lazy wash, head down, hind leg up. Perfect! Matagato took a stance – held it for a second, took another deep gasp of breath and jumped, holding on to the stick now with all of his legs for greater impact.

'Crippling cat-attack!' he yelled as he landed on the sleek tabby head. He drove in the spike with all his strength and followed the blow with his fangs, fully expecting the cat to collapse instantly into a dead heap on the path.

Mission accomplished!

However, to his great astonishment, Cleo merely continued the steady rhythm of her wash. Matagato, now sitting behind her ear, was paralysed with fright!

Now what?

Cleo, feeling a strange tickle on her head, flicked her ears a few times, thought about it for a second more, and feeling no relief, she scratched the tickle with a few rapid swipes of her rear paw. One extended claw hooked Matagato by his headband and jettisoned him in frozen state across the path and onto the grass, where he rolled into a ball at the feet of the horrified spiderlings.

In such a dangerous situation, he would normally have stayed in a ball, hidden by the long grass until danger was over. However, fearing for the safety of the spiderlings nearby, should the cat come searching for him, Matagato, without thought for his own safety, ran in the opposite direction towards the base of the apple tree, fully expecting the cat to pounce on him at any moment. He found a hiding place near the gnarled roots and fallen leaves but Cleopatra wasn't interested. She didn't even notice him and calmly continued her morning wash, the rasp of her sandpaper tongue breaking the silence that had fallen.

The disgrace of it!

Matagato was devastated. Not only had he failed to fulfil his mission, but all the spiderlings had been there to see him fail. How demoralising! He could never show his face again! Creeping further into the comforting darkness and hollow solitude of the tree, he made up his mind never to come out again. He had failed and had no choice now but to die the honourable death of a Samurai soldier! He would fall on his sword and die! Well – he would think about it.

When the spiderlings had recovered from the initial shock of this amazing spectacle, they all ran to the web school in the coal-bunker to find Amy, who came running to the scene at full speed. Seeing the cat, she edged cautiously around the roots of the tree, warning the spiderlings to keep their distance.

'Joe!' she called softly. 'Are you all right?' There was no answer so she crept closer. 'Please Joe. Come out of there. We can talk about this, can't we?'

Matagato's answer came from deep inside the tree and was very short. 'Talk? Oh yes! Let's talk! I failed – end of talk! Go away, Amy.'

Rosy Red started to cry. 'This is too sad,' she sobbed. 'Now we'll never see Matagato again. Life will be so boring without his Kung-Fu practice.'

'Don't be so selfish!' snapped Stephanie Silk. 'How can you even think about *our* lives being boring when poor Matagato is suffering so much?' Six great teardrops rolled down her face and fell onto the grass.

Miguel Dangally, suspecting that at any moment his small sister would join the other two and start to blubber, dashed off to his web, returning moments later with a small parcel wrapped in a shroud of silk. He gave it to Amy. It was his entire food stock.

'Is for Matagato,' he panted. 'A small fly and cricket snack for eating when he 'ungry.'

'I shall never eat again!' said the voice from the tree. 'Go away, all of you! The only thing left for me to do now is to starve myself to death or fall on my sword – well, my monkey stick – and die with dignity like a brave Samurai soldier.'

'You can't do that, Joe,' said Amy, who also watched far too much television through the lounge window. 'Samurais are Japanese warriors and Kung Fu is Chinese. You can't mix the two. It just wouldn't be right.'

Matagato did not answer. Amy sighed deeply, leaving the little web parcel at the entrance of the root cavity. She placed a feeler around Miguel, who turned bright pink and slowly squirmed away.

'That was a very kind thought Miguel, but perhaps we should leave him on his own for a bit to get over his disappointment. I think it might be a good idea if we don't mention this little incident to Sergeant Sparks or Minnie Money. I'm sure that Matagato will feel much better in an hour or two and it will be all forgotten.'

She led the little group of spiderlings away to the

climbing frame but they didn't feel in the mood for playing. The fine drizzle continued and the sky was slate grey, promising more of the same. All in all it had been a thoroughly miserable morning. Fortunately, there was the training session to look forward to later that day – if the weather cleared!

'Let's see if Stan Lawntidy has got anything new for us to play with,' suggested Stephanie. 'We might as well have a look. You never know – he might have found some of those little polystyrene balls. They were fun. Remember? At least it's nice and dry in the refuse store.'

The spiderlings did not share Stephanie's optimism but she was right about one thing – they would at least be out of the rain.

Stan and Karen Lawntidy

Stan and Karen Lawntidy were the proud owners of by far the best looking web in the garden. It was immaculate in order and impressive in design. Any odd threads of silk that were broken by the wind or disturbed by trapped insects, were immediately removed and renewed. Food reserves were neatly parcelled in silk and stored in the larder area. The double hammock that hung beneath the main web was beautifully woven for two, and was kept tidy both night and day.

The Lawntidy web hung in a narrow, cat-free zone between the greenhouse and the stone wall. Mrs. P also kept well away, as the area was overhung with thick ivy and housed many bugs and other creeping creatures.

Stan kept his garden refuse store on the short strip of ground under the web. Here he cleaned, sorted and listed any item found in the garden thought to be worthy of re-cycling. Different lengths of cocktail sticks lay in straight rows in order of size. Bits of cotton thread were wrapped in tissue paper and stacked in piles on ivy leaf shelves. There were small polystyrene balls, a large pile of bird feathers and a little mound of sand. Broken egg shells were stored one above the other on the stone base of the greenhouse, along with bits of copper wire, springs and very small safety pins.

'What's the point of keeping sand, Stan?' Karen had asked, after Stan had spent a whole day transporting it grain by grain to the store.

'You never know,' said Stan. 'It might come in useful one day.'

'And cocktail sticks? Only Joe Matagato has ever asked you for a cocktail stick in all the time we've lived here.'

'Might be a life saver! Who can say?'

'Cotton? Feathers? Who would ever need a feather? Life saver?'

'Naw, Karen. Cat bait!' Stan always pronounced 'no' as 'naw'.

'Cat bait?'

'Yes Karen, cat bait. Cats like birds and birds have feathers. Anything else?'

'No, I was just wondering – that's all. Look! Here come the spiderlings. They'll want something to play with.'

'There – you see? It's always useful to keep things.' Stan left the pile of sand and stepped forward eagerly to welcome the little group. 'And what can I do for you youngsters today?'

'We're bored!' said Hannah. 'Have you got any of those light-weight little balls?'

'I have indeed!' said Stan, with a meaningful sideways glance at Karen. 'But I think I can do better than that today. How about a helter-skelter?'

The spiderlings looked at each other, puzzled.

'We don't really know what that is,' said Hannah politely, 'but it sounds very interesting.'

'Follow me, please,' said Stan. 'You too Karen – I might need your help. Bring your bag!'

Stan led them to the back of the store where a wire spiral rested against the stone wall. At one time it had been attached to a small notebook that someone had left in the garden, but the paper had rotted away in the rain. Stan had needed the help of both Karen and Matagato to drag it to the store and prop it against the wall.

'I can't move it, so you'll have to play with it right here,' he told the spiderlings. 'But first I need to make sure that it's safe. We don't want any sharp bits.' He turned towards Karen and held out a hand. 'Eyes!' he said sharply. Karen opened her handbag and placed his glasses carefully but firmly in his open palm. He put them on and then his hand shot out again. 'Pliers!' he said. Karen had to fumble for the pliers as Stan waited. He peered at her over the top of his glasses, his lips pressed tightly together. 'Grease!' he said, handing her back the pliers. The grease was all ready in Karen's hand to pass to him. The spiderlings watched silently as they worked. At last he handed back the grease to Karen and stood back to inspect his creation.

'Did you used to be a brain surgeon, Mr. Lawntidy?' asked Hannah Silk, sweetly.

'And did you used to be a comedian, Miss Hannah?' said Stan, trying not to smile. 'Brain surgeon, perhaps not, but this is a good helter-skelter.'

'It's very good,' said Stephanie. 'But what do we *do* with it?'

'*Do* with it? What do you *do* with it? Well you helter-skelter down it of course!'

The spiderlings stared blankly and Stan raised his feelers impatiently. 'Karen!' he ordered. 'Climb up there and show the spiderlings how to helter-skelter.'

'No chance!' she retorted. 'You can just climb up there yourself! It was *your* idea!'

But Stan had no intention of trying it out himself. Instead he lifted Stephanie Silk and placed her gently at the top of the spiral.

'Wait there,' he said and dashed off, returning a moment later with a gold safety pin. 'Now thread the top of the spiral through the closed pin and hold on tightly to it. I'm going to push you to start you off.

Lift all your legs and just go with the flow. Ready?'

Stephanie braced herself and was ready to go but suddenly Stan remembered something else and dashed off, this time returning with a bottle cap which he dragged along the ground and placed just below the bottom end of the spiral.

'Help me to fill it with feathers – the really small ones,' he told the spiderlings, raising his eyebrows at Karen and mouthing the words 'life saver' to her.

He then skirted the wall and firmly planted all his legs on the wall beside the top of the spiral where Stephanie, still waiting to go, crouched for the off. Standing behind her and pulling her by the waist, he shouted 'Hold tight!' and pushed her in an anti-clockwise direction down the spiral. Squealing all the way, Stephanie swung out and round and round until she finally landed with a soft bump on the feather landing pad.

'Humungous!' she panted as she jumped out of the bottle cap and staggered away from the helter-skelter. The other spiderlings then rushed forward, all falling over each other in their eagerness to have a go.

'Just a moment,' said Stan, well pleased with the success of his invention and the good use of resources from his garden refuse store. 'We'll have an orderly queue at the base of the spiral and the safety pin will be transferred each time to the next in line. I'll stay at the top to operate the launch.'

The light drizzle turned to heavy rain, but the happy spiderlings, warm and dry under the thick ivy, spent most of the wet afternoon enjoying the new activity. Stan Lawntidy had also enjoyed the fun but finally declared that he was tired of being 'launch pad' and sent them all home.

'Save some energy,' he told them, 'for the training sessions – and The March.'

Sergeant Sparks
and the Training Session

The rain stopped at last. As planned, Sergeant Sparks met the Silk, Dangally and Red spiderlings for the training session behind the coal-bunker. It was a safe area, being too narrow and branch-entangled for Cleo or hungry birds to squeeze into.

First, having made sure that neither Mrs. P nor Cleo was in the garden, he marched them to the kitchen window where they peered through the glass at the dreaded bug-catcher. It lay on its side on the window ledge, with its sliding trap door open wide like a gaping mouth.

'Study it carefully,' he told them. The spiderlings stared at it but were quite unimpressed. It was nothing more than a plastic stick on a transparent box. They had been expecting something much more deadly and fearsome.

'But – that's not dangerous,' said Stephanie Silk. 'I wouldn't be afraid to walk into that now that I've seen it.'

Sergeant Sparks laughed.

'You wouldn't be walking into it, Miss Stephanie

Silk. Mrs. P would trap you in it in a flash – then she'd close the sliding door with you inside, probably crushing one or two of your legs.'

Stephanie winced.

'What would happen to her then?' whimpered Philpot Red, hoping that if it did happen, it would be to Stephanie and not him.

'Well – if she's still alive, she'll be taken across the main road to the vicarage,' said Sergeant Sparks. 'Not the end of the world, but getting back here could be quite difficult, especially if half her legs have been chopped off. Come on all of you! Back to the coal-bunker!'

The sergeant asked them to form a circle around a flat stone and they waited quietly for his instructions. Even Miguel Dangally kept a respectful silence, and tolerated, with great patience, the fierce stranglehold that his sister kept on one of his legs.

Sergeant Sparks studied them silently for a few moments, a strategy that ensured he had their full attention. There were fourteen of them altogether. He took out his notebook and ticked off their names one by one. First there were the five little Silks – Lucy, Stephanie, Hannah, Kat and Bex. Next were Miguel and Victoria Dangally. Then the sergeant ticked off the seven Reds, who were much bigger spiders – twins Philpot and Rico, Rosy their sister, Kio and

Siam and finally, Jade and Conor.

The sergeant carefully placed before them half a bird's eggshell, its dome upwards. Stan Lawntidy had supplied it. The sergeant climbed onto an overhanging branch of faded honeysuckle and positioned himself directly above them. Spinning a single strong thread of silk, he lowered himself onto the domed surface of the shell. Sticking the end of the thread to the shell with his special super glue, he then doubled it to make it stronger, by carefully climbing back up, spinning around the original thread as he went. Tugging this cord to test its strength, he nodded his approval and returned his attention to the fascinated group below him.

'Right!' he said. 'Behold the bug-catcher! Well – almost! Now that you've all seen this monstrosity on the kitchen windowsill, you'll see that it looks a bit like this, except that it's square and much bigger. However, the principle is the same. It consists of a handle, represented by my thread, and a dome, represented by the broken eggshell. I haven't got a trap door to slide across and that's a pity because the sliding door is the dangerous bit. Never mind – this bit of training will teach you how to move if the dome descends on you. You must learn to jump up and stay high inside the dome so that the door doesn't harm you when it slides across.' He pulled the silken threads until the eggshell lifted into the air. 'Now! Who will go first?'

He stared down at them, his lips pressed into a grim line. Eventually, Miguel Dangally freed himself from his sister's vice-like grip and stepped forward.

'I first!' he declared, anxious to get it over with.

'And I second!' said Victoria, but her voice wavered.

'Very good! Now watch carefully, everyone. When Miguel runs across the stone, I will drop the eggshell dome on top of him. Just imagine that I'm Mrs. P in a terrified panic. As the catcher descends on him, he must jump quickly into the uppermost part of the dome. If he doesn't do it at the precise time, the walls of the catcher will trap his legs. That's the first potential killer! The eggshell will not hurt him much if it hits him, but I assure you all, that the real bug-catcher will hurt a lot. It is much heavier than this, and when Mrs. P is nervous, she is not all that accurate. She often chops off legs without meaning to – and then of course she apologises because she's a C2 and doesn't want to hurt us.'

Sergeant Sparks mimicked Mrs. P's voice. 'Oh I'm so sorry, poor spider. I've cut off your leg but don't worry – you've got seven more.'

Only Miguel laughed, but more from nervousness than anything else. The others looked on silently and the sergeant gave his last piece of advice.

'As soon as you are in the dome – stay there! Don't try to run at this point because the second potential killer is the trap door closing! It could close on you as you try to escape! Are you ready, Miguel? You need to be running because that's what you'll be doing if Mrs. P is after you.'

Miguel nodded – too scared to speak. He prepared himself to run and trembled as he saw the great egg-shell dome rise above him. Sergeant Sparks gathered the silken threads until the dome reached a web-span's height. It swung ominously in the breeze. Miguel jumped on the spot for a moment or two and then he ran his weird jumping kind of run. What happened next was so fast that the spiderlings gasped and stepped back. The egg-shell dome came crashing down over Miguel as he reached the centre of the stone. He made such a mighty spring that he banged his head on the highest point inside the shell. Victoria held her breath. Where was he? Was he all right? She leaned forward to see if any severed legs protruded from the edge of the dome. Not one! The sergeant lifted the dome by its threads, and there was Miguel, sitting on the stone, all legs accounted for, grinning from ear to ear and rubbing his head while they all applauded him. He had done it!

'Well done lad!' said the sergeant from above. 'But stay high inside the dome next time – remember the sliding door! Next!'

Despite Miguel's success, all the spiderlings were still nervous and Vicky regretted her brave decision to go second. She glanced at her brother who was still bouncing up and down. Not wishing to appear cowardly, she suddenly ran towards the stone.

'Fogoonesek!' she said. 'Why all this fussing! Is just shell-egg! Stupid shell-egg! Do now! Do now!' Her voice rose to a screech.

The sergeant needed no second bidding as Victoria was already on the run. The shell fell quickly onto the squealing, already bouncing Vicky. She sprang lightly into the dome and hung there, her mouth open with surprise and joy. But as the sergeant lifted the shell again to let her out, she forgot to let go and both Vicky and eggshell swung into the air. The spiderlings held their breath. Was she hurt? A second later, her cheeky little face appeared upside-down from the rim of the swaying shell. She smiled, and spinning a single thread, she did a somersault in the air and performed a perfect descent. She landed elegantly at the feet of the flabbergasted spiderlings who applauded her enthusiastically. Taking a bow, she ran to Miguel, who beamed his approval and pride.

After that, the training session ran very smoothly. Even Rosy Red, the youngest member of the Red spider family, surprised them all by her skilful legwork and as the shell lifted, she jumped neatly onto the stone. She gave her audience a little pirouette followed by a curtsy using all eight legs. Then, completely overwhelmed by her own performance, she ran into her brother Rico's arms and burst into tears.

Sergeant Sparks was very pleased. All but one of them had passed the first stage of training. The exception was Philpot Red, the garden bully, who wouldn't even attempt the jump. When it was his turn, he suddenly started shaking all over.

'I don't need to do it,' he faltered. 'I'm sure I could do this perfectly so I don't need to prove it.'

'In that case you can show us a perfect example,' said the sergeant with a smug smile. The spiderlings glanced at each other knowingly.

'Go on Philpot,' said Stephanie Silk. 'We would all love to see how it *really* should be done.'

Philpot backed away, frantically searching in his bully's brain for excuses, but none would come. He knew that he would be branded a coward forever if he backed out, but the more he thought about it, the more terrifying it became.

'I *would* do it,' he stammered, still shaking, 'if someone would just hold the shell still while I jump.'

The spiderlings couldn't believe it and fell about with helpless laughter.

'Well, I hurt my leg this morning and I've got a really bad belly-ache,' he added, limping around in a circle and holding his stomach at the same time.

'Get on with it lad,' said Sergeant Sparks. 'My patience is running out. I can't hang up here all day waiting for you to run through a list of excuses. If little Vicky Dangally and Rosy Red can do it, I'm sure a big fellow like you should have no difficulty at all.'

All eyes were fixed on Philpot in the silence that followed. Then Rosy Red gave a great huff of impatience and placed her feeler arms on her hips. She wrinkled her nose in disgust. Having a family member turn against him was too much for Philpot. He backed off slowly and then turned, running off as fast as his legs would carry him. He even forgot to limp.

The sergeant sighed, swung to the ground and unfastened the web threads from the shell.

'Well done, all of you! Don't worry about Philpot. I've told you all many times before, that bullies are always cowards. We'll meet here again tomorrow for another training session if there's time, and then I think you'll all cope very well if you are unfortunate enough to come across Mrs. P's bug-catcher. Congratulations!'

The Grandees' Meeting

Later the same day, the Grandees, who were specially appointed leader spiders, held their net meeting at The Web Site, high in the upper branches of the apple tree.

Matagato was not there and Sergeant Sparks made a mental note of his absence. Matagato had only recently been elected as a Grandee, which was a great honour for one so young. He certainly should not have been foolish enough to be absent from a meeting so early in his Grandee career, especially such an important gathering as this one, headed by the General himself.

Minnie Money arrived a few minutes late, complaining about the height of The Web Site. Baby Frank clung to the top of her head like a hat, his legs covering her eyes so that she could hardly see.

'Do we have to be right up here? It's taken me fifteen minutes to climb up. We haven't *all* got long legs, you know,' she grumbled, giving the sergeant a list of the spiderling orphans in her care.

'I'm afraid so, Minnie, but I can organise a silk-thread lift for you if you like – and I'll haul you up myself. What more can I say? This is the only thick cluster of leaves remaining on the tree. We can't afford to be careless at this late date. If Mrs. P spots a large group of us in one place, then we're finished.'

'She'd probably have the tree chopped down and taken to the other side of the main road,' said the General and everyone, except Peter the Good, laughed.

'One should not jest about such things,' said Peter, frowning over the top of his half-frame spectacles.

Even as he spoke, there came a warning call from the garden gate. Karen Lawntidy was on duty to enable Peter to attend the meeting. She jangled the single communication web line once, to report an unidentified van in the drive. Vans always meant some kind of building work and could suggest potential danger.

The Grandees watched from their lofty perch as the stranger from the van opened the gate. Mrs. P came out of the house and they met on the gravel path beneath the apple tree. All eyes looked down suspiciously but not one of them was prepared for what happened next. The stranger suddenly grasped a thick lower branch of the apple tree and shook it repeatedly with all his strength. The tree shuddered.

The spiders, taken completely by surprise, were flung about in all directions, spinning webs rapidly as they fell. Stan Lawntidy was caught off guard and completely forgot to spin, landing with a crash on a lower branch of the tree. Minnie Money was so frightened that she anchored herself to one of the General's great legs. As soon as she realised what she had done, she shrieked and let go, only to roll under his great body and finally come to rest with a bump at the base of his boot. Her spectacles hung precariously from one ear and baby Frank clung tightly to the other.

'Are you all right, my dear?' asked the General, lifting her to her feet and gently helping her to adjust her spectacles.

'Perfectly, thank you,' she answered, her face quite pink with confusion, not having decided if she should feel embarrassed or honoured. 'What does it mean, General? Why would someone suddenly shake the tree like that? Is it a bad omen?'

'Maybe I shouldn't have made that joke about the tree. It was clearly a bad joke. There! He's going! No accounting for humans, Minnie. They do the strangest things. All we can do is be watchful. Perhaps he was just helping the last of the apples to fall. Perhaps he likes apples and was hoping that Mrs. P would give him some. Who knows? Shall we resume the meeting, ladies and gentlemen?'

Slightly bruised and certainly shaken, everyone eventually settled down again for the meeting.

The March was planned for the late afternoon of the following day. Each Grandee was allocated a building and a group of spiderlings. As she had expected, Minnie Money was allocated the house for the winter, with the Silk and Dangally orphans, accompanied by the sergeant, Matagato and Amy. Peter the Good was asked to take responsibility for the Red spider families in the garage. Stan and Karen Lawntidy were allocated the greenhouse with all the window spiders. The troops were ordered to help where necessary, and when the march was complete, they were told to occupy winter barracks in the coal-bunker.

'The march to the house will be by far the most dangerous of the marches,' said the General. 'I feel almost sure that we shall move tomorrow evening at dusk but I suggest that all spiders should meet me up here at The Web Site with their escorts in the late afternoon to receive last minute instructions. Spiders who are not allocated to the house will find the march relatively easy, as there are so many gaps and holes in both the garage and greenhouse. The house, unfortunately, is very well sealed, which is why I have allocated it to the smaller spiders, who will stand a much better chance of entry and survival. I'll see you all tomorrow!'

The General saluted them and then swung rapidly upwards to his hammock above The Web Site. He was very tired and planned to take an afternoon nap. Carefully removing all his boots, he placed them in a neat line. He loosened his tie and lay back on his pillows, made by Minnie Money. Closing all his eyes, the General tried hard not to think about The March, but it was impossible. *What a great responsibility it was!*

Miguel Dangally and the Search for Matagato

Amy was finding it very difficult to concentrate on the spiderlings' *Life Skills* class. It was hard for her to feel enthusiastic about teaching them how to stay safe, when her own very best friend was at that very moment in mortal danger. Matagato was still refusing to come out of hiding. Amy felt helpless and cross at the same time. The spiderlings, who were all very fond of Matagato, could not stop talking about the incident of the attempted cat kill. Eventually, Amy could bear their chatter no longer and forbade them to mention Matagato's name in the Spidergarten School, where her word was law. Today's lesson was about avoiding capture in the house by running up curtain folds or behind bookshelves. After five minutes, Miguel Dangally raised his feeler.

'*Señorita* Amy. Is very interesting what you say about 'iding in curtains but I 'ave important question about the life skills and it is this. 'Ow long can he live a spider without nothing to drink and eat?'

'*Without nothing* I do believe is a double negative, Miguel. I've told you about this before. You can say

without anything to eat or *with nothing to eat,*
but you can't say *without nothing*. Anyway, if
you're talking about Matagato, I've asked you not
to, so I'm going to be very cross if you continue.
Is that understood?'

'I not sure,' said Miguel, 'because my English she
is not so good already but very better than Vicky.
I no speak about this person Matagato who I no
allowed to say his name – O.K? I ask my question
about a good *amigo* of me who you not know. He is
very, very fat and want to get very, very thin. If he no
eat, 'ow long he live before he get thin and die?'

'And what is this friend's name Miguel? Do tell me!'

'My friend, him name is Harry the Spider. Him my
mate Harry.' Miguel beamed, pleased with himself
for managing to pronounce the 'H' in 'Harry', which
he normally left out.

Amy smiled, despite herself. Then she sighed and
said slowly.

'In that case, Matagato – otherwise known as Harry
the Spider – will live for a long time, Miguel. Don't
you worry! We shall soon have him out of hiding!
Now can we get on? I need to teach you about
avoiding dehydration during the winter and more
about the benefits of bookshelves. Don't look so
puzzled, Miguel. Dehydration means drying out and
it can be a fatal condition for house spiders during

winter, especially in houses which have central heating. It is very important that you all find a source of water and, if possible, a place which offers moist conditions. Normally, the bathroom is a good place, and there are two in the house so we are lucky. Attics are good as well because of condensation. We'll now move on to the skill of hiding. Bookshelves make very useful temporary hiding places if...'

Amy's soft voice droned on, but Miguel was not listening. He was thinking about Matagato. As soon as the lesson was over, he slipped away quickly to avoid his sister, and hurried to the base of the tree. He crept into the hollow of the roots and called, 'Matagato! Is me, Miguel! I need some 'elp with the Kung Fu.'

Silence.

'Matagato! Please! You must 'elp me. Philpot Red want to give me a big poonyatatho on my 'ead and I very afraid. You know what is a big poonyatatho? You know? Is a big fist, and 'im fist is more big than my body. What you think Matagato? Matagato?'

Silence.

Miguel crept further into the gap, wondering how Matagato, who was much bigger, had managed to squeeze into such a small space. Suddenly, he came to the end of the hollow. It was empty! The small food parcel that Miguel had given to Amy earlier that day, lay untouched on the ground. Matagato was not there! Miguel was so surprised, that he didn't even feel foolish about talking to himself. Picking up the parcel, and full of joy that Matagato had emerged, he dashed over to the window, fully expecting to find him in his usual place below the jutting bay.

But Matagato was not there either. The southern monkey stick lay discarded on the gravel where Matagato had left it when he failed in his mission. Miguel dragged it with great difficulty and hid it behind a flowerpot.

He scratched his head, more worried now than before. It became obvious to him that Matagato had found a new and better hiding place so that no-one would bother him while he died of starvation. Miguel sat on a stone and sadly shook his head. Matagato was like a big brother to him and had helped him many times, especially when Philpot Red was a problem. Now Matagato himself was in need of help. Miguel got up, determined that he was not going to let his friend down.

'I *will* find him!' he vowed and set off on a search. Fifteen minutes later, having still not found Matagato, he climbed the rotary washing line and swung gently to and fro on a single thread of silk, in deep meditation. *Where could Matagato be? He wouldn't want to be anywhere near the cat. That*

much was certain. But the cat went everywhere. She
patrolled the garden every day, sniffing here and
there to make sure that no other animal had invaded
her territory. Maybe the greenhouse!

Without turning his head, Miguel looked through
the open greenhouse door with a rear eye, but the
first thing he noticed inside was Cleopatra, lying fast
asleep on the shelf among the withered and dying
tomato and cucumber plants. So much for that idea!

Where would Cleopatra not go?

Miguel thought so hard that his head began to hurt,
but suddenly he knew! He knew without any trace
of doubt where Matagato was hiding! He was so
excited that he twirled around on his single thread,
and almost strangled himself.

'Why I not think of it before?' he choked. 'This
cat is so stupid and fat that she never go where all
normal cat go. She always wait for the door of the
'ouse to open for her, because she too fat and lazy for
the cat flapping thing. She afraid to be stuck forever.
Matagato is in the cat flapping. I sure!'

Miguel jumped down as fast as he could spin and
made for the porch door. He felt just a little nervous
at the thought of partly entering the house, which
was forbidden territory. Minnie Money would be
furious if she found out, but it was a matter of great
urgency that Matagato should be saved. It was up

to him, Miguel Dangally of Spain, to save him. He punched his chest with pride but slowed down as he approached the flap, uncertain of how he would get in. Using his feelers, he measured the gap between the swinging plastic door and its casing. Creeping forwards, he was just about to squeeze through, when the voice of Minnie Money from somewhere above made him jump on all eight legs and stop in his tracks.

'Miguel Dangally! What in heaven's name are you doing down there?'

Miguel was rooted to the spot. Now he really was in trouble. At first he did not dare to look up. He searched his brain frantically for a good excuse but his mind turned blank. Reluctantly, he raised his head to face Minnie's wrath. But where was Minnie? He couldn't see her; not on the window ledge; not on the guttering and not on the roof of the porch either. She was of course very small but this was ridiculous. Had he imagined it? Then he heard a stifled giggle and Hannah Silk's cheeky face appeared over the guttering.

'Well? I'm waiting for an explanation!' she said in a perfect imitation of Minnie. She grinned from ear to ear. Miguel was relieved but not very pleased.

'Very, very funny! You frighten me outside of my skin. Why you 'ere? Is not allowed coming 'ere.'

'I could well ask you the very same thing. You were going into the house, weren't you?' Hannah accused him. 'Come on…tell Auntie Hannah.'

'Of course no,' Miguel answered truthfully. 'I am looking only at this door they call stable door. Is not door to stable because inside is no 'orse. English is very interesting thing.' He decided that it would not be wise to tell Hannah of his plan to find and help Matagato. It was after all a delicate matter and Matagato would not want to be badgered by the whole crowd of spiderlings. Miguel clambered up beside Hannah, planning to return to the cat flap later, when he was alone. Together they scaled the wall and crossed the gravel path to the apple tree, Hannah chatting merrily all the while.

'Did you know that Stan Lawntidy hurt his legs in the apple tree today? Someone came into the garden and shook the tree hard while the net meeting was going on in The Web Site. Stan had a fall.'

'But why shook the tree? There are no more many apples. Are you sure about this?' Miguel wondered if Matagato had moved hiding place for this reason.

'Of course I am sure. Peter the Good told me, and he never tells lies, unlike some spiders I know! He said that Minnie Money held onto the General's leg. Just imagine that!'

'The General's leg? That is so funny. Did he say

Are you pulling my leg?' And they both fell onto their backs laughing. 'You know,' Miguel added between giggles, 'that in Spain we say *Are you pulling my hair?'*

'That's weird! You're very strange aren't you, Miguel? And sometimes you speak funny – but I like it. I suppose you think that we speak funny as well. I feel very sorry for you because you will never be able to go home again. You tell us so many interesting things about Spain that I'm sure you must be very homesick.'

'Is true, but what is the point to break my 'ead about this? Of course I miss the warm of the Spanish sunshine, and English insects is taste very different, but I am 'ere and this I no can change. In Spain we have a famous saying – *Don't cry new tears over old things!* I cry many times when I first 'ere, but no more. Little by little I forget.' Miguel, feeling a sudden, tight restriction in his throat, thought it was time to change the subject. 'Come with me. I can make a very good web trampoline. No, better still! You get all the others and I meet with they at the coal-bunker in one hour. OK?'

'You're on! I'll round them up. Cool! A trampoline!' And Hannah was just about to run off, leaving Miguel his chance to return to the cat-flap, when she noticed the food parcel still clutched in his hand.

'Miguel! Why are you carrying a food parcel?' she asked.

Miguel hesitated before answering. He hated telling lies.

'Is for sharing with a friend,' he said. *That wasn't a lie!*

Hannah licked her lips.

'I'm a friend – you can share with me if you like.'

'No gracias, amiga! You very kind to offer, but this friend is the more 'ungry than you. Perhaps another day – OK?' And he was gone in a flash.

Hannah shook her head, disappointed, but then she remembered the promise of the trampoline and scurried off in the direction of the climbing frame to find the others.

Miguel, meanwhile, had returned to the cat-flap. Not hesitating this time at the swinging door, he squeezed his body into the gap between flap and outside frame. It was dark inside – the ideal hideout for a spider, especially as the cat had never used it. Bedraggled threads of broken web, dry leaf skeletons and tufts of fur from previous cats long dead, cluttered the area. At first the only inhabitants appeared to be an empty woodlouse carcass and a frozen-in-time harvester. Miguel switched on his night vision and called softly.

'Matagato! Are you 'ere?' *Silence*! He called

again and from deep in one of the dark corners, Matagato answered.

'Miguel! Go away – please!'

Miguel was jubilant.

'Oh Matagato – thank for the goodness I find you at last. Is very important that you come out. You see – Amy is very, very sick and…'

'Nice try Miguel. Now go away if you don't mind. I'm busy.'

Miguel could tell that this was not going to be easy. He would need more time.

'OK my friend. I will go if you eat this food,' he said stubbornly. 'And if you no eat, I will go to the Sergeant Sparks and I tell him Matagato is 'iding in the cat flapping.'

'You wouldn't dare,' said Matagato. 'I would flatten you and feed you to the birds...or the cat!'

'I think no, *amigo*. I sure that you is liking me very, very much. Why you no eat this? Then for the moment, I will keep my big *boca*, that means my big mouth, very shut. I keep 'ow you say – shtum – for the moment.'

In reality, Matagato was very hungry and as Miguel opened his little web parcel and offered him the juicy crane fly, his mouth watered. He reached down and took the food eagerly, tasting it with the special sensors on his feet.

'OK! I'll eat it, but only because I don't want the sergeant here. He'll only tell the General and then I'm in big trouble. Now clear off kid. Deal done!'

Miguel waited stubbornly. Matagato had not started to eat.

'Look! You can watch me if you like.' He started to inject digestive juices into the food as the delighted Miguel bounced on the spot.

'Mmm, very tasty! My favourite! And fresh! You must have just caught it.'

'No, I no tell lie! It the same food I bring when you disappear into tree, after you lose fight to kill … Oh, *mama mia*, what I say?' Miguel realised his lack of tact in mentioning the taboo subject of the cat attack. He finished lamely, feeling all of Matagato's eyes boring angrily into him. He thought quickly.

'When you squash cat's ear,' he said hastily.

'Squash cat's ear?'

'Yes, she limping now, very bad.'

'She's limping – because I squashed her *ear?* Get out of here kid before I…'

'I come back with more food later,' Miguel said as he jumped backwards, thinking that a hasty exit would be wise at this precise moment.

'Just a moment, my friend. Not so fast! How is my Amy?' asked Matagato casually, his mouth full of fly juice.

'Oh she fine.' Miguel stopped his mouth with both feelers. Too late!

'But I thought you said she was sick.'

'Is true I say that but I tell lie. I am very big liar but is no my fault. Is faulting my English. I want to say Amy sad, not sick. Then I get confuse with sad and sick so I tell big lie. But is lie from the heart – I promise! A very white lie! Amy – she very, very sad and this is true. She cry all the time with the eyes very sad and wet. And she be more sadder when she no find you in tree. Why you no come out with me? Come *amigo.*'

'Don't you *amigo* me you little spidersqueak. Just because I ate your fly. Now clear off and leave me alone.'

Miguel went happily. He had achieved his first aim, which was to get Matagato to eat. He was convinced that eventually he would achieve his second aim, which was to get him out of hiding. Glancing back as he left, he could just make out the shadow of Matagato doing press-ups in the corner.

It was a very good sign!

The Trampoline

Hannah had spread the word about the trampoline and a small group of spiderlings now waited impatiently at the base of the climbing frame. Bex and Kat attempted to make their own trampoline at the top of the frame but they failed miserably and ended up covered with each other's sticky silk.

'Are you quite sure he said he would be here in one hour?' said Stephanie Silk. She had been trying to console Victoria Dangally, who could not understand how her brother had managed to escape from the classroom without her. She hated to be separated from him for even a moment and clung desperately to Stephanie's hand, stamping all four legs in misery.

'One hour,' Hannah repeated. 'But I'm not sure if he meant a Spanish hour or an English hour.'

'There's no difference! How stupid!' said Bex.

'Of course there is! Everyone knows that in Spain one hour might mean two and that *mañana* – that's Spanish for 'tomorrow' – well, that could mean next week. Miguel told me and he should know.'

'Is true! Is true!' piped Victoria. 'But not today, because here is he!' She ran happily towards her brother, who sauntered across the garden path with a huge grin on his face. He was so pleased with himself that he forgot his usual reserve and held out his feeler arms to Victoria, who ran towards him eagerly. He swung her around and around until she begged him to stop. Releasing her suddenly, they both staggered dizzily onto the grass, collapsing together in a happy heap. For Vicky, such affection from her brother almost made the separation worthwhile.

Miguel led the spiderlings to the safe area behind the coal-bunker and started to work on the scaffolding for his trampoline. The well-pruned ivy that backed onto the side wall of the garage provided the slender supports he needed for a frame. It was entangled enough to provide safety not only from the cat but also from birds, who were great enemies. Fortunately, at this time of year there were so many berries around that the birds welcomed the different diet and mostly left the spiders alone.

Miguel worked at great speed while the others watched, fascinated by the skill of his intricate weaving. He had greased his legs before starting so that he would not stick to the threads and be trapped like a common fly in his own web.

'That is a delicate miracle of design and technology,' said Hannah. 'Do you know that spider silk is the strongest natural fibre known to humans?

It can stretch three times its own length and it does not dissolve in water. If we could only tell the humans our secret – how to make it – just imagine how it could change the world!'

'Who told you that?' asked Lucy Longlegs.

'Amy told me,' replied Hannah. 'She knows everything. I think I'll be a teacher one day.'

'It's a pity then that we *can't* teach humans how to make spider silk,' said Lucy. 'We could come to an agreement. We tell them our secret if they agree not to torture us.'

'Oh well! That will never happen,' said Bex. 'But look! You can talk about how to make spider silk if you like, Hannah. I'd rather jump on it. Come on! It's finished!'

The magnificent trampoline was indeed ready and Miguel stood back to admire his work. It had cost him eighteen metres of silk and almost an hour of his time, but it was worth it. After a few amendments here and there, he was satisfied.

'I try it first!' he said, and climbed on cautiously while the others watched, now impatient to jump on. After a few tentative bounces, he could tell that it was strong enough for them all to use.

'Yes! It good!' he yelled. 'It work! It work! Grease your legs and bodies so that you no stick and let's bounce!'

They all greased up and climbed on, falling over each other in their excitement. At that precise moment, the beat of a Spanish dance drifted out over the garden from the kitchen window of the cottage. Mrs. P always played Spanish music while she was cooking dinner. The little group were soon bouncing to the beat and squealing with laughter. There was such a commotion that the Red spiderlings, who were playing nearby, came to see what was happening.

'That's a really cool trampoline, Miguel,' said Conor. 'Can we have a go?'

'Of course! Why I would say no? But you must wait one moment please until the small ones have finish, because they small and you big!' said Miguel, stretching his legs to make himself appear taller.

'That's a good idea,' said Rico Red. 'We don't want to hurt the little ones. We can wait Miguel. There's no hurry.'

But Philpot, his twin, had no intention of waiting. He pushed his brother aside and puffed himself up.

'Get your crowd off, Dangally! I want to get on *right now. Right now!* You got it?'

On the trampoline, the Silks stopped bouncing, sensing trouble. Miguel hopped to the edge and looked down at Philpot. He smiled at the bully.

'I think no, Philpot. Listen to your brother Rico. He say sensible thing – no stupid thing.'

'Are you saying that I'm stupid, you half-pint?'

'I think so, yes – but no is your fault that you stupid. I feel the big sorry for you because you can only be bully with little creatures but you afraid of eggshell. You life must be sad and very alone.'

'Sad? Sad? Are you calling me sad? Get down here this minute Dangally and I'll show you what sad is. Sad is you, squashed to a pulp.'

Miguel sighed. Then he raised a feeler and stopped to listen. The dance music of a dramatic Spanish *pasodoble* was now being played in the kitchen.

'All right. I come down. But I no fight with you. I teach you to dance the *pasodoble* instead. Ok?'

'Dance? Dance? Me dance? You'll be the one dancing all right – in pain! You'll be dancing for weeks Dangally. Ha! Ha! Ha! Dance! That's really funny!' Philpot turned to his brother and sister but they were not laughing.

'Stop now Philpot!' said Rico, feeling very ashamed of his twin. 'I'm not with you on this.'

'And neither am I,' added Rosy. 'Sometimes Philpot, you are quite pathetic – *and* sad!'

'And the rest of us aren't with you either,' said Jade. 'Ignore him, Miguel. We can wait for our go.'

Kio and Siam stood nearby, feeling uncomfortable and helpless. Miguel jumped to the ground and stood before his opponent, who was more than twice his size. The anxious faces of the Silks peered down from the edge of the trampoline as Miguel took an elegant Spanish dance pose, one feeler on his hip, the other high above his head.

'Listen to the beat of the music, Philpot. Four beats to the bar. The *pasodoble* is very easy. We will count – one, two, three and…'

But on the count of four, Philpot lunged forward. At that precise moment, Miguel sprang with a single movement to the left and Philpot's full weight crashed down onto the ground.

'Ole! Ole!' yelled Victoria from the edge of the trampoline.

Miguel returned to his dancing stance and smiled down sweetly at Philpot. 'Oh, I forget to say you – when count four you must change the direction. Come – you need more practice my friend, but you soon learn. Please no worry!'

Philpot, gasping to regain his breath and turning red in the face, staggered to his feet.

'One, two,' counted Miguel, springing to the right this time on the count of three because he knew that Philpot would attack early. True enough, on the count of three, the enraged bully pounced again, fists raised. He gave a great roar and launched into space, falling on his knees with a resounding thud.

'Oh *madre mia!*' Miguel said to him. 'I must learn

to count good in English. Always I make the confuse with three and four. I so sorry. Come! We try again – no? First we take rest – you look a bit tired.'

Miguel relaxed against a stone, all legs crossed. He beckoned to Philpot to join him, patting the stone beside him.

Philpot, furious now and beginning to feel stupid, did not quite join him. He ran directly towards Miguel, four long arms spread widely. He aimed to squash him against the stone, aware and prepared this time that Miguel could move to the left or to the right. With his body and four evenly spaced fists, he planned to pulverise Miguel left, right and centre. What he didn't account for was that jumping spiders could jump in all directions. Miguel simply sprang in an upward direction at the last moment and Philpot smashed his head, body and four fists with full force into the stone. He fell to the ground, completely stunned. Miguel landed on Philpot's back, shaking his head sadly.

'I sorry again. I think maybe dancing is no for you. Oh look you poor 'ead! Why you do that to 'ead? We play a different game – no? You like tag? We play tag!'

But Philpot was not in the mood for tag at that precise moment. His body hurt all over and his pride hurt even more.

'You are one dead spider! I'll be back!' he hissed when he had found his voice. Then the bully sloped off, muttering revenge and nursing his injuries. Miguel called after him.

'*Si,* you come back. We no be long on trampoline. You no like dance very much but trampoline is good – and easy. You can to play trampoline later with other Reds – no?' There was no answer.

Miguel sprang back onto the trampoline and soon the Silk spiderlings were again happily bouncing and bumping each other in time to the music, all thoughts of Philpot and the dreaded Autumn March forgotten. The smallest spiders had no control over their own legs as the bigger ones bounced. They could only laugh uncontrollably and go where the bouncing took them. After a while, the Reds, except Philpot, took their turn on the trampoline while the Silks regained their breath.

At dusk, Minnie Money called the Silks in for supper. They were so tired when bedtime came that they all climbed into their small hammocks and fell asleep without the usual arguments. All that is, except Miguel Dangally, who stayed awake long into the night, trying to think of a plan to get Matagato out of the cat flap in time for The March.

A Sleepless Night

After The Web Site meeting, Sergeant Steve Sparks returned to his web home in the electric meter box.

The sergeant was worried. *Something wasn't right!*

He was pleased with his 'Allocations to Buildings List' because he was going to escort Minnie Money and the Silks. It wasn't that! He was also confident that the spiderlings would cope well if confronted with the bug-catcher. So it wasn't that! His troops were well trained and ready for action, so it wasn't that either. He hung beneath his web for a while, swaying to and fro while he tried to analyse his doubts. Finally, after much thought, he decided that it was the tree-shaking incident that had bothered him. Why would someone come into the garden, shake the tree, talk to Mrs. P and then go off again? It was puzzling!

He tried to think of a logical explanation. Humans normally shook trees to make the apples fall, but the fruit season was over and the apples were all gone, even the rotten ones that had fallen onto the grass, attracting dozens of wasps. Mrs. P had called her daughter to clear the fermenting mass away. In Mrs. P's estimation, wasps were almost as bad as spiders and solely designed to spoil her enjoyment of the garden in autumn. No, it couldn't be that. Not apples! Not to test the branches for making a swing either because there was already a swing hanging from the climbing frame.

The sergeant climbed up to his hammock that hung between two electric meter dials and stretched out to think.

His uneasy mind wandered back to the previous year and the famous 'catastrophe.' He had, as always, planned very well, but on the morning of last year's March, the continuous heavy rain had caused the river that ran from the Quantock Hills to the sea, to burst its banks and flood the village. The cottage garden was near the river and was the first to be flooded. The spiders allocated to the garage had just completed their march and were safe in the roof space, just moments before the water level in the garage rose high. However, the spiders marching towards the coal-bunker and greenhouse were taken completely unawares by the sudden tide of floodwater. Many of them died.

The house spiders were still in the tree and were cut off by the flood water. They watched helplessly as their friends on the ground were swept away by the angry, swirling water. High in the tree, they were too far away to reach any building and there wasn't even a breeze to carry an anchor web-line to the house. They were trapped. That apple tree again! Last year nature had locked them out. But it was nature's timing that also decreed the day of The March. It had not made sense.

It had been a very difficult and worrying time, saved solely by the sergeant's skill in problem solving. He remembered that Matagato, the television fanatic, had told him once that humans could swing like spiders from tree to tree by means of a kind of pulley-line attached to both ends of the distance to be covered. Spiders did something similar – an essential part of web building – but they relied on the wind to carry them with the first thread of web.

The distance between house and tree was quite substantial and without even a breath of air travelling in that direction, it seemed an impossible problem to solve. The sergeant had hung on his anchor thread, waiting for a breeze. The others puffed with all their might to get him swinging. Nothing! It was then that the sergeant had a great idea! If the heaviest spiders attached themselves to the line alongside him to give it extra weight and the others pushed, they could perhaps swing toward the house like humans. He lengthened his thread, and the General and Peter the

Good climbed on. All the other spiders pushed. Little by little the strong thread swung wider and wider until finally, when it was as near to the house as possible, the sergeant shot out an extra thread of silk which carried them above the guttering of the roof.

'Jump!' he had yelled and they had all leapt forward, landing in a heap in a torrent of rain-water in the gutter, but still hanging on tightly to the line.

The other house spiders had then crawled across the thread to the safety of the eaves of the house and into the attic where it was dry.

That was the catastrophe of last year!

What would this year's problems be?

The sergeant sighed and turned over in his silken hammock. It was no use worrying about it. All they could do was to plan as carefully as possible and leave the rest to nature. And so he finally drifted into fitful sleep.

It seemed to him that he had only been asleep a short while when suddenly it was morning. But what a morning! A great brightness flooded into the meter box through the gap in the badly fitted doors.

'Oh no!' he said, struggling to get up. 'This can't be true. Please! Someone tell me this can't be true.'

From his hammock, he could see that the garden was covered in deep, deep snow.

'Snow?' he yelled. 'Snow? In October? It can't be!'

But it *was* snow. Snow everywhere. Not only on the ground but covering the garage, the tree, the climbing frame and the huge camellia plant.

'How can this be?' he shouted in disbelief. 'The General is never wrong. He would have sniffed snow a mile away. Oh my gosh! The Silks and Minnie Money! They must be buried alive in the camellia pot.' The sergeant knew that he must act quickly. He must free them – dig them out. But the more he tried, the less he was able to move. He was tied to his hammock by invisible threads. All his legs moved but he wasn't getting anywhere. Who had tied him to his hammock? He struggled in vain to break free. He had to save Minnie and her spiderlings at all costs. He made one last effort to free himself and this time, finding no resistance, almost fell head over heels out of his hammock. The snow had disappeared! It was dark night! With his night vision full on, he peered out. No snow! No brightness! Just the dark shadow of the apple tree against a slate grey sky!

It had all been a bad dream, brought on, no doubt, by worrying about The March.

The panic subsided, but it took some time before he could relax. He lay in his hammock, thinking for a long time about the following day, praying that all would go smoothly.

While Sergeant Sparks worried about The March,

Miguel Dangally tossed and turned, pondering on various plans to entice Matagato out of the cat flap. He knew that he had less than twenty-four hours to achieve his goal. He sat up in his hammock, rested four elbows on four knees and peered around the web. Minnie Money was snoring gently. She never found it difficult to sleep. The four Silk girls with Vicky Dangally and Lucy Longlegs were all together in one large hammock. Stephanie, Hannah and Lucy were awake, whispering to each other so that they didn't wake up Minnie. Bex and Kat, like Minnie, were sound asleep, their arms tightly locked around each other.

Miguel Dangally thought hard about his problem, but discarded various solutions as they all involved telling lies. He knew that he was not a good liar and that Matagato would see right through him. The image of his friend doing press-ups in the cat flap gave him hope. Why was Matagato exercising if he intended to die? Body conditioning and fitness was an integral part of Kung Fu. It was obvious that if Matagato had started to eat and was exercising, then he had no intention of starving himself. He had not taken much coaxing to eat the crane fly Miguel had brought him.

Food! The answer was in food.

Miguel wondered if he could entice Matagato out of the flap with the promise of a gourmet meal – the juiciest morsels he could find. He could describe the food in mouth-watering detail until Matagato wouldn't be able to resist any longer. Yes – that was it! But what if Matagato *did* resist? What then? Miguel would have to sacrifice himself to stay with Matagato and join him on his hunger strike. That would make Matagato feel very guilty. Yes – that was a better idea!

Miguel imagined himself getting thinner and thinner on the cold floor of the cat flap; the hero who died in an attempt to save his friend.   He pictured being found by the sergeant and the General as he breathed his last breath. How proud they would be of his bravery and loyalty to Matagato. Then Miguel imagined how sad Vicky would be – no, not sad – broken-hearted, an orphan alone in a country that was not her own, abandoned by her only living relative – her brother.

Miguel wavered – then much to his relief, he remembered that The March would take place the next day. There was not enough time for such a sacrifice. All the spiders would be on The March and there would be no one left to find their thin dead bodies. He decided against the idea of dying and suddenly felt very relieved – and then bored with the whole situation. Tomorrow was another day.

He would think about it tomorrow.

He turned over and fell asleep straight away.

The Day of The March

The General was the first one to wake on the day of The March. He ate a hearty breakfast of midges on housefly and dressed carefully, humming quietly to himself. It promised to be a beautiful autumn day but he sensed that, despite the cloudless sky, it would rain that evening. This did not worry him unduly because, by then, all the garden spiders would be safely housed for the winter. The spiderlings had been fully trained and the Grandees knew the procedure. Everything was ready! What could possibly go wrong?

From his web, high in the apple tree, the General gazed down on the garden. He smiled to himself as he watched his little community of garden spiders slowly waking up to this new and important day. Sergeant Sparks stood at the entrance of the meter box, stretching all arms and legs in the pale morning sunshine. The Silks were having breakfast at the camellia plant. On the other side of the lawn, Rico and Rosy Red were bouncing on what was left of Miguel Dangally's trampoline. Philpot Red sat sulking on the ground below them. The other Reds,

Kio and Siam were playing tag with Conor and Jade on the circular patio.

Beneath the bay window, Amy was busy making food parcels and dismantling the web she shared with Matagato. The General wondered why she looked so sad and he was therefore pleased to see Peter the Good approaching her. Peter was always jolly and had the special gift of cheering people up.

Stan and Karen Lawntidy were having an argument. Stan was repairing their home web and stacking all the things he had recycled from the garden in tidy piles so that everything was in pristine order. He had made a silken sack in which he placed a few things that might be useful for The March in an emergency – some food parcels, a small feather and a bit of cotton wool. Karen stood behind him, waving all four arms in frustration. Her voice carried on the still air.

'For goodness sake Stan – we're leaving today! What's the point of tidying up? None of it will be here when we get back in the spring. We'll have to start all over again. Come on lad, let's have an untidy day and enjoy it. It could be fun.' She gave him a playful look but Stan ignored her. Routine was routine! No one could say that he left his home ugly (which Stan pronounced *ooglay*).

'I can't stand an ooglay place Karen – you knaw

that! There's nowt worse than ooglay!'

The General chuckled as he put on his hat. It might be a good idea to have a stroll around to say a personal farewell to everyone. As he left his web, he caught sight of Miguel Dangally circling the garden. Miguel stopped suddenly under the bay window and disappeared behind a flower pot. Moments later he emerged with a small piece of cocktail stick strapped to his back with silk. All his knees buckled under the weight of it. The General scratched his head in puzzlement. *What's that young scamp up to now?*

The General liked the Spanish spiderlings. They brought variety to the community and had shared some great Spanish ideas, like the trampoline. They were different. They had large, beautiful front eyes, and made the others laugh with their amusing accents and their odd little step - jump way of moving. *Wish I could do that – would be very useful.* And the General tried. Step… jump! Step… jump! He stumbled and almost fell, but tried again. *Maybe I could do it with a bit more practice.* Step… jump! He heard a titter of laughter and looked down. Minnie Money was watching him from the camellia plant.

The General raised one glove to his mouth to cover a little embarrassed cough, at the same time hastily brushing the front of his jacket with the three other gloved hands. Minnie quickly averted her eyes and hastily disappeared beneath the shell of the stone tortoise with the broken head, where she collapsed in girlish giggles.

The sound of Mrs. P unlocking the back door in the porch to let Cleopatra out, reminded all the spiders in the garden of the danger ahead. Today they couldn't hide in their high safe webs. Today was different. Today they had to venture out. The General waited in the tree until Cleo was out of the garden before he began his farewell circuit. Cleo wasn't very interested in small spiders like the Silks, but the General was large and therefore well worth the hunt. He knew he was safe in the tree, as she was too fat and lazy to climb it. He made himself comfortable, knowing that it might be a long wait.

His attention returned to Miguel Dangally who was now struggling up the wall of the porch beneath the cat flap. *Now what is Miguel doing near the 'no go' area?* He rested an elbow on his knee and watched until Miguel disappeared behind the rose trellis. *I'll speak to that young scallywag later and also find out why he's carrying that stick.* He continued watching the trellis, waiting for Miguel to emerge. Cleo began to patrol the garden, sniffing here and there for traces of any animals that might have dared to enter her territory during the night, especially the large ginger cat from next door that she hated with a vengeance.

Miguel Dangally, unaware that the General was watching him, was *en route* to Matagato's hide-out in the cat flap. The stick in its silken cords was still firmly fixed on his back. When Cleo had appeared, Miguel had slipped behind the trellis for safety. The three parcels of food and the stick weighed him down so much that his climb was painfully slow. He welcomed the break in the trellis.

What would he say to Matagato? How could he convince him to come out of isolation? How he hated that cat! He glared at her as she disappeared into the greenhouse, her fat underbelly wobbling from side to side as she walked away. Then, with a hasty glance both ways to make sure that no one could see him, Miguel picked up his gifts for Matagato, struggled into the cat flap and switched on his night vision.

Expecting to find Matagato in the same far corner, Miguel was surprised and delighted to find him practising a Kung Fu form in the middle of the cat flap floor. He had cleared the woodlouse skeleton and other rubble to one side and was speeding from one corner to another, all legs and arms in action. Miguel knew not to interrupt a form until it had finished and Matagato had performed the final salute, ending as always in the exact starting point. It was impressive!

When I get Matagato out of here, I must get him to teach me this art, Miguel thought.

He applauded Matagato with four hands.

'*Ole! Ole!* Very, very well, *amigo!*' said Miguel, taking Matagato so much by surprise that he turned into attack mode. Miguel dropped the food parcels and despite the weight of the cocktail stick, retreated in a single jump, bashing his head on the flap and falling in a heap on the pile of rubble. The transparent woodlouse shell was draped around his head.

'*Por favor amigo!*' he cried. 'Don't kill me! I bring you present!'

Matagato helped him up.

'You might warn me next time kid! I could have pulverised you – but that's a formidable jump, especially with my heavy stick strapped to your back. It *is* my stick, isn't it? Yes – a very impressive jump! But what do you want this time?'

'OK. I knock next time but it no will be necessary because this the last time I come. We all moving today – The March – you remember? I will never see you again in this whole my life, my friend – and you will never see your Amy in this whole your life also.' A large tear plopped from Miguel's biggest eye onto one of the food parcels. He wiped it away angrily and busied himself removing the stick from his back.

Matagato frowned. 'Ah yes… The March… what is…?' Miguel's hopes rose and he answered quickly.

'What is time? At dusk! You with the sergeant

and the Silks – and the Dangallys of Spain – that me and Vicky.'

'I know that *chico*. Not what is the *time*? What is for dinner?' Miguel tried not to show his disappointment. He must succeed today!

'So you come – no?' he ventured.

'I might – later – not now. Where's the grub?'

Miguel began to un-wrap the parcels eagerly.

'Crane fly for starter, house fly for main course and midge for pudding. We meeting at The Web Site later. Nobody miss you yet – only Amy, so if you there, she very happy – and me very happy either.'

'I'll think about it,' said Matagato, 'but I have to get revenge on that cat somehow – I'll think about it. Thanks for the grub and the stick. You're a good kid.'

It was enough for Miguel. He was jubilant.

'Don't you worry about cat. I have big plans for revenge on cat. I 'elp you. You think I just small jumping spider but I have big, big tickle. No one know this about small Spanish jumping spider because I never tickle in this country. My tickle not very itch human but cat smaller than human so tickle very itch cat – not kill cat but itch very much. Cat scratch and scratch and itch get worser and worser. Together we make cat pay, no worry. *Adios amigo* – I see you later.' And leaving Matagato scratching his head in confusion, Miguel disappeared through the crack in the flap. Once in the fresh air, he clambered through the trellis and jumped, bounced, and cartwheeled down the wall.

'Si! Si! Si!' he shouted, his arms and legs flying in all directions.

The General, who had been watching the trellis all this time, saw Miguel's strange performance and was puzzled.

'That is one very peculiar arachnid!' he said aloud. 'Spidernalities are obviously very different in Spain.' He noticed that Miguel was not carrying the parcels and the stick. *He's hiding food in the trellis! That's very interesting! Now why would he do that? And what did he want that stick for?* Moments after, Miguel was lost from view behind the leaves of the camellia.

The General's attention was diverted to Cleopatra who was trying to climb the wall into the churchyard. It was an amusing sight. She was so fat and unsure of herself that it took a lot of tail end wobbling and aborted attempts before she finally gained enough confidence to really go for it. Finally, she risked it and disappeared over the wall. The General descended the apple tree on a single bungee line and began his farewell tour of the garden. Wherever he went, he was aware of an air of nervousness and excitement and tried to reassure the spiders that all would be well.

Miguel Dangally returned to the web in the camellia plant where Minnie was giving the spiderlings last minute instructions.

'And where have you been, young Miguel?' she said. Miguel hesitated.

'I visit my friend,' he said honestly. Hannah gave him a sidelong look.

'Have you been sharing food again Miguel?' she asked.

'Of course,' he replied. 'My friend no catching very much lately. I think is really coming winter and the flies all gone to hot country.'

Hannah smiled at him and raised her eyebrows.

'Really?' she said.

Minnie warned the spiderlings that they only had a short time to play. She reminded them of the assembly at The Web Site.

'Don't go far,' she said. 'I don't want to have to come looking for you.'

The March?

Later that day, at about an hour before dusk, the community of spiders emerged from all corners of the garden and began the long climb to The Web Site at the top of the apple tree. Had Mrs. P been in the garden, she would have thought her worst nightmare had come true, but she was in the kitchen preparing fish for her dinner. The usual medley of Spanish music rang out from the open kitchen door. Cleo had returned and was now draped across the kitchen windowsill, watching Mrs. P and hoping for a few titbits of fish, instead of the usual dry biscuits.

In The Web Site, the General, flanked by his troops, waited patiently for everyone to arrive. There was an atmosphere of nervous tension surrounding the adult spiders and the spiderlings sensed it. They fidgeted and whispered to each other under the watchful eye of Minnie Money, whose formidable stare reminded them to behave. Miguel Dangally watched anxiously for Matagato, hoping earnestly that he would appear, but there was no sign of him.

Miguel was not the only one missing Matagato's presence. Amy sat apart from the others, gazing

107

down on the garden, knowing in her heart that he would not come. It was getting too late! The thought of a long, lonely winter without him was unbearable. She had looked everywhere for him since discovering that he was no longer at the base of the tree. Where was he? Was he all right? She concluded that he must have left the garden altogether and this made her feel hurt and more than a little angry. How could he do this to her? She sighed deeply and tried to concentrate on the meeting.

The General rose to his feet and tapped his stick against a branch of the tree. They were all there except for Peter the Good, who was on look-out, and of course, Matagato.

'Ladies and gentlemen, boys and girls,' he began, but he got no further. The Web Site communication thread jangled as the alarm was given by Peter the Good.

'Abandon all window webs! Abandon all…' Peter stopped, suddenly realising his mistake. There were no spiders in window webs. They were all in The Web Site.

'I beg your pardon. I mean… Alarm! Alarm!' he yelled, not knowing what else to say. All eyes from The Web Site lowered to the main gate in confusion. What looked like a window cleaner's ladder appeared above the gate. *Two window cleans within two days? Impossible!*

They watched anxiously as the ladder, supported by a man who was also carrying a huge metal gadget in his other arm, struggled into the garden. The ladder swayed along the garden path and was rested with a jolt on one side of the apple tree. Mrs. P's head appeared at the kitchen window.

'Oh it's you!' she said. 'I thought you'd changed your mind when it got so late.'

'Won't take me long missus. I'll have this down in a jiffy,' the man replied, pushing the ladder firmly against the tree and jerking the cord on the vicious looking gadget, which roared with power. In The Web Site, the spiders watched in terror, turning to the General for guidance. The General raised his arms for order.

'Wait! I'm not sure what's happening here. Don't panic, anyone!' But the man scaled the ladder in moments and was soon within metres of the top branch where the spiders were gathered.

'I've never known of an apple tree with woodworm before,' the man yelled down to Mrs. P, 'but it's hollow and will cut through easily.' He began to saw through the highest branch.

It was the very branch that housed The Web Site.

'Red Alert!' commanded the General, now recovering from his shock and disbelief. The troops sprang into action, dividing themselves between the groups of astounded spiders.

'Bungee! Now! Scatter!' they ordered.

The community of spiders needed no further bidding. They jumped! The group of Silk spiderlings, who had been gathered close to Sergeant Sparks and Minnie Money, all dived at the same time, spinnerets working at top speed. The top branch keeled over even as they swung. They landed in front of the kitchen door and ran, not knowing what to do next. The sawn branch of the apple tree suddenly crashed onto the ground behind them and they fled, together with Philpot, Rosy and Stan Lawntidy to the only spot available – the open kitchen door. Seconds later, Amy joined them, clutching Baby Frank tightly with all four arms.

Mrs. P and Cleo were watching the scene from the window. As the first branch came crashing down, Cleo ran upstairs with fright but Mrs. P stayed where she was, saddened by the destruction of the beautiful tree. As the anxious little group scampered through the doorway, something flew overhead and landed in a ball with a soft thud in the middle of the kitchen floor.

They couldn't believe their eyes!

It was the General!

Trapped!

The General had remained behind like a true leader and had jumped to a lower branch until the last spider had fled to safety, but he had left it too late for himself. The branch had fallen and he was catapulted into the air and through the open kitchen door. The Silk and Red spiders, remembering their training, immediately fled behind the cooker which was the only dark accessible place, but the General lay in the middle of the floor without moving, his hat and stick lying at his feet.

'He's dead! He's dead!' cried Stephanie Silk with a sob that set off all the other spiderlings. Minnie Money began to run towards him.

'Oh no! Oh no! Not the General!' she wept.

Sergeant Sparks stopped her at the gap between the cooker and the next unit.

'No wait,' he said. 'Look! He's moving. The fall has stunned him but he's all right.'

And sure enough, he stirred. Unfortunately, at that moment Mrs. P turned away from the window to attend to her cooking. She saw the General immediately and jumped back in fright, barely stifling a scream by clapping her hand over her mouth. She backed away towards the window, not taking her eyes off him. Her right arm reached behind her, groping for the dreaded bug-catcher and what happened next was so rapid that the terrified onlookers gasped all together in dismay.

In a flash, the bug-catcher crashed down on the dazed General and the plastic door was closed, trapping one of his legs. Mrs. P turned off the heat on the cooker and fled into the garden, leaving the bug-catcher on the floor, jumping over branches and making little whimpering noises as she went.

'Mr. Bailey! Mr. Bailey! There's a huge spider in my kitchen. You must come and get it for me! Please Mr. Bailey – I beg you!'

'Not now missus! I'm in full swing. I'll get it for you later. Won't bite you know and there are thousands more up here.' He chuckled.

'This is not a laughing matter young man! Oh forget it! I'll go and get my daughter! She's probably next door at her friend's house.' She stormed off, springing over the mounds of branches strewn over the garden, still in a state of fright and imagining thousands of spiders beneath her feet. She wasn't far wrong. Under the debris, garden spiders were escaping in all directions. The March had been converted from a well-planned manoeuvre to a frenzied evacuation.

Back in the kitchen, the General had recovered slightly, but he soon realised that he was trapped. He stared out forlornly from the transparent door of the bug-catcher. He felt dreadful. He had lost his hat and stick in flight, he had a headache and his leg hurt badly. In her haste, Mrs. P had left the bug-catcher on its side and the General's leg stuck out limply from the closed door.

Sergeant Sparks was the first to emerge from beside the cooker.

'All out!' he yelled as soon as he knew that Mrs. P had fled. 'All out and help me to push up that door! You too Philpot Red!' Philpot, who had been trying to hide behind his sister, joined the others reluctantly. And how they pushed, but to no avail. The door would not budge.

'What are we going to do?' wailed Minnie. 'Even if Mrs. P takes him across the main road, he's injured badly and won't be able to get back. He'll be run over – I know it!'

The sergeant tried to console her.

'He does have plenty of other legs, you know, Minnie. That's not the problem. The problem is that she might accidentally injure him further. Come on, everyone – let's try again,' he said. 'After three and give it everything you've got.'

But it was impossible. Although the door moved up slightly on each push, the moment it was released, it dropped back down on the General's leg, causing him to wince with the pain.

'We have to wedge the door open somehow. Stan, do you happen to have brought any kind of stick in your emergency pack?' Stan's face fell. All that careful planning and when he most needed it, he was ill prepared! He shook his head, feeling very embarrassed.

Miguel Dangally suddenly started to jump and cartwheel on the spot.

'I 'ave it! I 'ave it! Wait one moment please! The southern monkey stick of course!'

'This is no time to play around with monkeys, Miguel. Calm down and let's think – but fast – time is running out.'

'No! I not play! I serious! Please – all wait 'ere. I fast!'

And he sped towards the cat flap in a series of hops, skips and jumps.

Matagato was asleep in his camping hammock on the other side of the flap, oblivious to all that had happened. Miguel, without thinking, sprang onto his chest and he awoke with a start, ready to attack.

'What the…?' he began, but Miguel sprang aside to

avoid the blow.

'Listen me please! The tree coming down and everyone run for life. We all in 'ouse, in kitchen. The General in bug-catching thing. She leg falling off and …she – no, he ask for you…'

Miguel could sense that cunning measures were needed to get Matagato moving fast. This was not a good time for honesty.

'The General say to getting Joe Matagato – he the most strong spider of all spiders. Tell him he needing fast. Tell him to bringing monkey stick!'

Miguel paused to catch his breath.

'What about Amy? Is she all right?'

'No – she stuck behind cooker – she very, very afraid,' Miguel lied again.

Matagato shook his head to clear away the cobwebs, grabbed the stick and then moved so fast that Miguel could not keep up with him, even though he jumped the whole way.

A few moments later, Matagato arrived at the sorry scene. He saluted the General.

'Matagato – with monkey stick, Sir!' he said, through the plastic of the bug-catcher.

When the sergeant saw the cocktail stick, he knew there might be a chance to save the General. The others stood ready for his orders.

'Ok! Now let's all push again – you too Matagato.

When we get the door moving – push the cocktail – um – monkey stick into the gap to hold it open. Then we can lever the stick to release the pressure on the General's leg.'

After the count of three, they all pushed again, and this time Matagato thrust the stick into the gap. It worked. Using the stick as a lever, their joint strength slowly widened the trapdoor a centimetre. The small Silks, Matagato and Amy squeezed through the gap and into the bug-catcher so that they could push up the stick from the other side.

Suddenly there was a scream from Kat Silk that sent Philpot Red running back to the safety of the cooker. The sudden loss of Philpot's weight caused the sergeant to fall. The stick slipped into the bug-catcher and the door dropped behind it. Matagato, Amy, Miguel, Stephanie, Hannah and Vicky, all toppled backwards into the bug-catcher. They were now prisoners along with the General.

As they peered out helplessly, they understood why Kat had screamed. The spiders outside the bug-catcher were fleeing to the safety of the cooker, Philpot Red being the first through the gap. The sergeant stayed only long enough to point to the dining room door. 'The cat! Watch out!' he yelled.

Cleo had returned to the kitchen and was now creeping towards the bug-catcher – ears alert, eyes

round, rear end swaying, tail up, and body ready
to pounce.

Inside the bug-catcher, the General and the others
stared out in disbelief. Cleo crept forward very
slowly, her eyes fixed on the bug-catcher. She knew
she had seen movement inside!

'Don't move!' whispered Matagato. 'Don't
even breathe!'

But Cleo's paw had already begun to investigate.
Claws extended, she rolled the bug-catcher
over, causing a gasp of fear among the group of
spiderlings inside who tumbled over each other. Cleo
touched the General's protruding leg very gently, and
it took all his courage and concentration not to move
it. Sergeant Sparks ran out from behind the cooker
and bravely performed a little dance in the hope of
distracting the cat, but her eyes were fixed on the
General. She made a strange little 'Mac! Mac! Mac!'
sound and examined the door with her paw and nose.
She lay on her side and little by little, she managed
to slide the door until it was open enough to get her
front paw in. Her head was too big to enter but her
nose quivered a few centimetres from where the
spiders lay in a heap. They all held their breath and
slowly, slowly backed up to the furthest corner. The
General, wincing, slowly withdrew his injured leg
and shielded them with his huge body. This was the

end – they all knew it! Little Vicky Dangally closed all her eyes tightly and clung to her brother. The Silk girls crouched under the General's legs. Matagato, Amy and Miguel peered over his shoulder. Cleo's paw spread widely like a fan, treading air. The needle sharp claws shot out from their sheaths.

She was just about to hook the General when, without any warning, Miguel Dangally made a mighty jump from the General's shoulder and landed on Cleo's tender nose. He jumped furiously on the spot, trying to stamp all his feet at once. Cleo glared at him, cross-eyed and distracted.

'Now Matagato! Now!' shouted Miguel, injecting Cleo's nose with the famous 'tickle' he had boasted of earlier to Matagato.

Matagato sprang over the General's shoulder and wedged his stick lengthways between the digits of the wide spread paw, which revealed a soft fleshy area beneath. Cleo, distracted by a sudden itching sensation on her nose, suddenly felt the stick tickling between her claws and thinking it to be the huge juicy spider she was hunting, she closed her paw tightly to trap it. The cocktail stick, lying sideways between her claws made its mark and Cleo stabbed herself – twice! Miguel, all his legs shaking like jelly, hopped swiftly back to the General's shoulder.

There was a furious yowl of pain and a hissing

shower of spit fell onto the spiders as Cleo sprang back in surprise. She withdrew her paw, hooking the bug-catcher with her extended claws and turning it over again. She licked the sore area to remove the offending stick which flew into the air, but the stinging continued. Now her nose started to itch badly. Her tail bushed up, her ears flattened and her hackles rose. A moment later, she shot out of the kitchen at full speed.

The spiderlings fled through the partly open door of the bug-catcher to the safety of the cooker, hugging each other in relief when they realised that they were safe. Matagato grabbed his stick as he ran.

What none of them realised was that the General was still trapped. The gap in the door of the bug-catcher was wide enough for the smaller spiders to crawl through but too narrow for the General to escape. He tried to breathe in and squeeze through, but it was impossible.

The sound of the garden gate opening made his heart sink. *Oh no, now Mrs. P is back! I'm doomed!*

But it was not Mrs. P entering the garden – it was Addie, her daughter. When she saw the huge mass of branches strewn across the grass, she stepped back in surprise.

'Jumping catfish!' she cried, pointing in disbelief at the space where the tree had been. 'What's going on?

Hey – why are you killing our tree?'

'I'm not killing it girl. It's as dead as a dodo!
I've never seen woodworm like this in an apple
tree before, and I've felled a few trees in my lifetime
I can tell you. The trunk is completely hollow.
The first bit of high wind would have sent this one
crashing down on your house. Very dangerous! Be
careful you don't scratch yourself on these branches.
Your mother's looking for you by the way.'

Addie skirted around the garden, amazed at the
amount of debris on the ground. Dumping her school
bag on the patio table, she went into the kitchen.
The first thing she saw was the bug-catcher on the
floor. Then she saw the General struggling to get out.

'Oh you poor thing!' she cried. 'What's my mother
been up to now?'

She fell to her knees in front of the catcher and
gently opened the door. The General hesitated, not
quite sure whether he could trust her.

'Come on, little fellow,' she said. 'I won't hurt you'.
Little fellow? Little fellow? The General, despite
his fear, puffed himself up and advanced. He knew
that he had an audience. From the safety of the
cooker, the other spiders were now aware that he
had been left behind and were watching the scene
with bated breath.

Addie gazed at the General adoringly, holding out

her hand.

'You are so pretty! How could anyone be afraid of you or want to hurt you? Come on! Out you come! Oh, your poor little leg is hurt! Don't tell me. I know who did that to you but she didn't mean to hurt you – she's just afraid you see.'

The General winced, but not from the pain in his leg. He mustered up his worse scowl! *Pretty? Pretty? One thing he was not was – pretty!* He glanced towards the cooker, hoping that the others had not heard, and then strode out defiantly onto the girl's hand. She lifted him to within centimetres of her face and he glared at her fiercely with all his eyes.

Addie studied him closely. 'What I don't understand is why you came into the kitchen in the first place. You must know what she's like by now. I'd like to keep you as a pet but there's no chance with someone like my mother around. Anyway, you probably wouldn't want to be a pet, would you?'

The General straightened seven of his eight legs in order to appear taller. *This gets worse! 'Little fellow' and 'pretty' is bad enough, but 'pet' really is too much! You can go off people you know!* He stamped his feet to show his disapproval but Addie did not notice. She was distracted by the sound of the garden gate.

Her mother!

'Uh – Uh! Danger!' she told him.

Glancing quickly around the kitchen, she then took the General to exactly where he wanted to go – to the gap behind the cooker. Very gently, she lowered her hand and let him go.

'Quick!' she said. 'Hide in there for the time being. I'll open the kitchen window for you later when it's dark so you can escape. Good luck, handsome!'

The General glowed. He liked handsome much better, especially as it was said within earshot of the others. He glanced back at the girl. *More people like her on the planet would be a wonderful thing.*

Safe!

Seconds later, Mrs. P appeared at the kitchen door, a little out of breath. Cleo, hearing her owner, also returned to the kitchen and sprang up to her usual place on the windowsill, licking her stinging paw and rubbing it over her nose which itched badly. Mrs. P stayed at the door, afraid to go in.

'You're here already,' she said to Addie. 'I've been looking for you everywhere. We must have passed each other. Have you seen…?' She stopped and stared at the empty bug-catcher on the floor. 'There's a monster spider in there – isn't there?'

'No – there's nothing in there, Mum. It's empty!' said Addie, truthfully.

'Oh no – don't tell me it's escaped! It must be here somewhere. Help me pull out the cooker. It must have gone behind it.'

The spiderlings held their breath. Not again! They had thought the worst was over.

Mrs. P started to struggle with the cooker but suddenly she caught sight of Cleo who was still washing her stinging paw and itching nose. Mrs. P knew that Cleo usually washed when she had eaten, and it wasn't Cleo's suppertime yet.

'Oh no!' she said, staring at Cleo. 'It's not behind the cooker. I know where it is. Please tell me that she hasn't eaten it?' There was a pause while Mrs. P looked closer at Cleo. 'She *has* eaten it! Oh you *bad* girl, Cleo! Oh, poor spider! You know I hate to kill spiders. My Granny always said, "If you want to live and thrive, let the spiders stay alive!" Oh you bad girl! You *bad* girl! No supper for *you* tonight – and it's your favourite – fish! Out! Go on! Out!'

Cleo's ears flattened and for the third time that day, she ran out of the kitchen, confused and hurt. Hurt both physically and emotionally. She hadn't had a good day at all!

The spiders behind the cooker fell about laughing, but more at their own relief than at Cleo's misfortune. How different it would have been if Cleo had really eaten the General. It was a horrible and sobering thought!

Minnie Money, who had watched the whole dramatic scene helplessly from the safety of the gap, now rushed to the General's side to attend to his injured leg. Spinning furiously, she ordered him to keep still while she wrapped a silken support around the swollen area.

'It'll be fine, just a scratch,' he said, brushing down his jacket. 'I've clearly got much more important things to do. For example, where's that young Kung Fu maniac and that scamp Dangally?'

Matagato and the other spiderlings pushed Miguel forward. He was bursting with the success of his joint action with Matagato back in the bug-catcher. The General placed a heavy hand on his shoulder that almost flattened him to the ground.

'Young man – what you did back there took great courage. You Matagato, did no more than I would expect from a Grandee, but well done anyway. But this lad is a spiderling. He risked his life for others and his bravery deserves a just reward!' The General carefully removed one of his medals and pinned it onto Miguel's t-shirt. The weight of it almost stretched Miguel's shirt to his knees. The General then placed one feeler on Miguel's shoulder.

'I now bestow upon you the greatest honour! From now on you hold the title of 'Grandee', an honour never before given to a spiderling. You have more than earned it. This could have been our worst catastrophe yet.' There was a moment of hushed silence. Minnie Money wiped away a tear of pride. Miguel beamed and saluted the General.

'Gracias Señor! I very honoured,' he said. They all clapped and congratulated him. Miguel looked at Matagato, who winked.

The General sat down wearily.

'I must leave you all as soon as it's dark. My duty lies in the garden now – I must see what I can do to help the others. You're all safe here until Mrs. P goes to bed. Use the exit at the back of the cooker and then go up the wall to approach the kitchen loft door where you should be able to squeeze through. Good luck to you all!'

The General suddenly noticed Philpot Red who was still shaking with fear at the back of the cooker.

'You! Red! You can do me the honour of going out there to retrieve my hat and stick! You're a coward, boy! Like all bullies! I shall make it my personal duty to see that you receive some thorough training. The sergeant will remind me next year. Jump to it Red! You and your sister will come with me – we need to find your brother Rico and the rest of your family.'

Philpot Red felt cornered. He was too scared to obey the General but even more terrified to disobey. His sister Rosy gave him a disgusted push and he crawled out, hugging the floor like a baby spiderling. He got the hat and stick, and ran back to the others, squealing with fright as he went. The General shook his head sadly, put on his hat and settled down to wait for darkness.

Stan Lawntidy approached him and saluted.

'Permission to leave the house with you Sir!' he

said. 'I'm worried about Karen. We were separated when The Web Site fell.'

'Permission granted,' said the General, 'but we must wait.'

An hour or so later, after testing his wounded leg, the General stood and addressed the other spiders.

'Until next year then! We must all hope for a mild winter and a wet spring. Then who knows? Even I might live for another year – like you Madam!' He took Minnie Money's hand and bowed deeply. Then he double saluted all the others, nodded briefly at Stan Lawntidy, hooked Rosy Red onto his shoulder and was gone. Moments later, the newly recruited house spiders saw them at the kitchen window which had been opened as promised by young Addie. Philpot Red tagged behind the General and Stan Lawntidy, staying as close as he dared.

Catastrophe?

Later that evening found them all safely housed for the winter in the loft above the cottage kitchen. It was the perfect place for spiders and completely safe from cats and people. Mrs. P would never climb up there among the cobwebs.

The spiderlings were in very high spirits. They explored the new space and found lots of interesting areas to play in. The loft was crammed with junk. There were crates and old suitcases, broken toys, an old doll's house and a slide for children. But by far the most exciting find was a wooden model of a gypsy caravan, complete with little carved windows and a set of tiny steps leading to a stable door. It was pale yellow and had beautifully scrolled designs on the outside painted in red, yellow, blue and green. Inside there was a living space, completely furnished with bunks, cupboards with opening drawers, a black stove and little fluffy rugs. An arched doorway led to a separate area containing a miniature bed, covered with a pretty blanket.

'Wow!' said Kat Silk. 'Do you think the sergeant would let us spin our sleeping hammocks in here?'

'We could have it as our house and keep our web parcels in this little drawer – look – it's open!' added Bex.

'Amy could teach us in here,' said Lucy Longlegs, bouncing on one of the bunks. 'Let's go and ask'.

At the other end of the loft, Matagato paced to and fro. Like everyone, he was very tired, but there was something very important that he had to do before thinking about sleep. Amy, with baby Frank clinging to her back, was trying to unpack food parcels that she had brought with her to feed the spiderlings. She glanced up as Matagato approached but quickly lowered her eyes again and continued unfolding the food. Matagato lifted the baby onto his shoulder to make it easier for her to move.

'Can I help you, Amy?' Matagato asked cautiously.

Amy glared at him. 'No thank you. I can manage very well without you – just as I have these last few days.'

'Amy – you don't understand. That vicious cat killed my friend! I was the only friend that Rowly had. I know she was unfriendly, spiteful, lazy, deceitful and vindictive but there had to be some good in her somewhere. She didn't deserve to be tormented and chewed to pieces by a cat. Just think about it for a moment!'

'That's the law of nature!' retorted Amy. 'It could happen to any one of us. You didn't have to hide yourself away – to die! Just think about *that*!'

Matagato thought about it. This wasn't going to be as easy as he had thought.

'What if it had been *you* that was eaten? It could just as easily have been you. What then?' he asked.

'I'm far too skinny!' she answered. 'Cleo wouldn't have been interested. Rowly was round – and juicy! This stupid mission to kill the cat will eventually be the end of you. Why can't you be satisfied that tonight the cat is not only hungry but also suffering a very sore nose. Tough as you are, you would never have been able to kill her. Never!'

Matagato saw his way out and smiled. 'So if I tell you that the mission is over forever – and if I apologise for leaving you lonely – will you give me a hug and say that we are friends again?'

'I might,' she said, turning her back on him, 'but I would need time to think about it.'

Matagato folded two pairs of arms and whistled quietly to himself. Then he peeped over her shoulder to see her face. Baby Frank copied him. Amy tried not to smile but it was impossible. Matagato hugged her tightly with all four arms and danced her around and around the pile of food parcels. Baby Frank clung on tightly to Matagato's head-band.

A broad, happy smile lit up Amy's face. Matagato handed her the baby and did a double cartwheel. Then he took the southern monkey stick from where it rested against the wall of the attic.

'I'll get rid of this,' he said, 'through the gap in the eaves.' He was just about to push it through when Amy stopped him.

'No, don't throw it away, Joe. It saved our lives – remember? Anyway, it will be something to show our children one day.' She glanced at baby Frank. 'Let's keep it as a reminder.'

The March of the Autumn Spiders was over for another year – and what a march it had turned out to be! It was certainly one they would all remember for a long time. On the chimney pot of the house, a solitary, huge spider surveyed the garden. General A. P. Crawly sighed with relief. Through the secret signals of the spider world, he knew that everyone was safe! Limping slightly, he headed in the direction of his own winter hiding-place in the garage.

In the attic above the kitchen, the spiderlings got ready for bed. Their new hammocks lay beneath a small temporary web that Sergeant Sparks had made for them in the caravan. As they were about to drop off to sleep, Miguel, still clutching the General's medal, suddenly sat up in his hammock and

132

scratched his head.

'Please! Something I no understand. Only one thing!'

'What is it Miguel?' came a sleepy reply from Hannah.

'Well – where is Stroffee?'

'Oh, not now, Miguel! Go to sleep! Stroffee? What's Stroffee?'

'Is my question. Is what I ask. Where is Stroffee?'

'What kind of Stroffee are we talking about here, Miguel?' asked a confused and sleepy Hannah.

'Where the cat come from?'

'Which cat are we talking about, Miguel?'

'I don't know which cat. The cat of Stroffee.'

'The cat of Stroffee? The cat of Stroffee? Oh, you mean the Ca–ta–strophe?'

'*Si* – cat of Stroffee. All day – everyone talk about the cat of Stroffee. What is?'

There was a pause while all the sleepy spiderlings thought about it. Then Stephanie's infectious giggle started them all off. A short giggle followed by a pause and then a longer giggle until the others started to join in. Eventually there was laughter from everyone, getting louder and louder by the minute. From outside the caravan, even Minnie Money tittered, and then Sergeant Sparks started to chuckle. Matagato and Amy laughed so much that they fell out of their hammocks. Every time they tried to stop laughing, Hannah said, 'Catastrophe!' and Miguel answered.

'Yes. Cat of Stroffee. That right. Why you repeat everything I say? What? What I say now? Why you all laugh?'